RUNAWAY LOVE

When Emma flees to Leigh Manor to escape the pain of a broken romance, she finds that life there as a secretary to Alex Baron is not as simple as she anticipated. An unfortunate encounter between herself, Alex and a bull heralds the start of a fiery relationship. And what is the mystery behind the charming façade of Blake, Alex's assistant? As Emma's new job gets off to a rocky start, she soon finds herself wondering who she can trust — and whether coming to Leigh Manor was a good idea . . .

FAY WENTWORTH

RUNAWAY
LOVE

Complete and Unabridged

LINFORD
Leicester

First published in Great Britain in 2016

First Linford Edition
published 2017

The names, characters and incidents portrayed
in this book are the work of the author's imagi-
nation. Any resemblance to actual persons, living
or dead, is entirely coincidental.

A catalogue record for this book is available
from the British Library.

ISBN 978–1–4448–3367–6

Published by
F. A. Thorpe (Publishing)
Anstey, Leicestershire

Set by Words & Graphics Ltd.
Anstey, Leicestershire
Printed and bound in Great Britain by
T. J. International Ltd., Padstow, Cornwall

This book is printed on acid-free paper

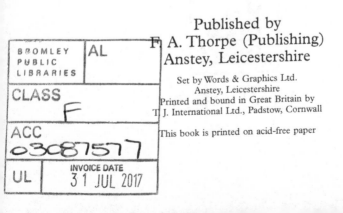

1

'Emma, you can't leave! How on earth will I manage?' Tony Merriman paced angrily behind his desk.

'I must, Tony. I'm sorry. I can't stay in London.' Emma stood and faced her employer, her green eyes beseeching. 'Please try to understand.'

'All I understand is that Frank Lander, the bastard, is depriving me of the best secretary I've ever had!'

Emma instinctively rubbed her ringless engagement finger. 'Miss Frobisher at the employment agency said she'd find someone suitable . . . '

'You've spoken to her — before telling me?' Tony rounded on Emma, his eyes sparking blue ice. 'Don't you think I should have been the first to know?'

'I knew you'd try and dissuade me.' Emma gave a wry smile.

'Too right! You love your job here, you're brilliant. You know every client, every financial deal . . . How can you do this to me?' He raked his hands through his dark hair.

Emma stood her ground. 'I have to get away, Tony. I've made up my mind.'

'You're just being stubborn and selfish, leaving me in the lurch because you can't handle a louse like Frank.'

'I can't,' Emma agreed. 'I need some space — time to get my head back together. Surely you can see that, Tony?'

'No, I can't! I thought you had more gumption. Letting a man like that drive you away . . . '

'Then you're not the friend I thought you were!' Emma felt anger bubbling. 'If you were, you'd understand. We've worked together long enough. Anyway, I'm going. I've already got another job.'

'You have?' Tony stopped in front of her. 'Where?'

'Herefordshire.'

'Good grief, *Herefordshire*? In *February*? Why on earth there?'

'It sounds interesting. And Herefordshire is a beautiful county. A complete change.'

'That's putting it mildly! Miss Frobisher to the rescue again, I presume?' His voice was sarcastic.

Emma stared at him, her expression grim. The last thing she wanted was to part on bad terms. But she had already accepted the job, and her replacement was starting next week. She felt guilty about not telling Tony first, but after the trauma with Frank, she couldn't face another lengthy confrontation. And Tony was reacting exactly as she had anticipated.

'Tony, please, accept my decision. Let's not quarrel.'

Grudgingly, Tony put his hands on her shoulders and gazed down into her troubled eyes. He brushed an auburn curl from her forehead and sighed. 'I'm sorry, Emma. But I'm devastated.'

'I know. But no one's indispensable.'

'You are!'

Tony wasn't to be appeased, and Emma left with a heavy heart.

★   ★   ★

Now here she was, standing on a dank platform in the pouring rain and wondering what on earth had possessed her to run so far away. She looked round. A young mother leaned against a dripping wall whilst her toddler played in a dirty puddle. There was no one to meet Emma. Taking a deep breath, she picked up her case and headed for the exit.

The car park appeared deserted. She heard the squeal of brakes. A muddy Range Rover pulled to a stop and a man jumped down. He was wearing wellingtons and was muffled in an anorak; all Emma could see was damp brown waves straggling on his forehead above hazel eyes.

'Blake Rowan.' He held out his hand. 'You must be Emma Marsden. Jump in.'

She eyed the vehicle and glanced down at her slim skirt. He grinned and held open the door. As she took a step up, he unceremoniously pushed her from the rear. Emma suppressed a sharp retort and gave him a cool glance as he climbed in the driver's seat.

'You've not been to Herefordshire before?' Blake started the engine and reversed onto the road.

'Oh yes,' Emma replied, 'when I was a child. My uncle farmed here and we spent our summer holidays with him.' She was looking out at the soggy fields and mud-churned scenery.

Blake chuckled. 'The countryside in summer is slightly more attractive!'

Emma laughed. 'So I realise. How far is Leigh Manor?'

'Another twenty minutes or so, depending on how many tractors we meet. This is Kestleigh.' He waved his arm at the straggle of cottages either side the narrow road. 'I'm the farm manager, by the way. Alex Baron owns Leigh Manor, but he's away on business at the moment.'

'Oh?' Emma was startled.

'A sudden trip,' Blake explained. 'He'll be back tomorrow. I have instructions to show you around. Then, when he returns, you'll know the setup and can get on without delay.'

'I see,' Emma murmured. 'What exactly does the job entail?'

'Mr Baron is diversifying.' Blake grinned. 'Income from farming is going downhill and he's decided to turn Leigh Manor into a tourist attraction.'

'Sounds a good idea.'

'Leigh Manor has several hundred acres,' Blake continued. 'Enough to accommodate his prize cattle and landscape the gardens. The outbuildings are in the process of being converted into a café and gift shop. He's also set up a craft centre for visitors to watch craftsmen in situ — a very popular idea at the moment. The whole concept goes under the banner of 'Leigh Leisure'. We're opening to the public in March, and Alex needs someone to run the day-to-day business and do the accounts and so on; generally to keep a close eye on progress. He was trained in business finance; he's very astute when it comes to making money.'

There was a slight edge to Blake's voice and Emma looked at him sharply, but his smile belied any criticism.

Blake swerved off the road and turned into a lane. 'We're here,' he said proudly, and drew to a halt in a spurt of gravel.

Leigh Manor was impressive. Grey-stoned, it stretched the length of a paved courtyard. Long, latticed windows glistened in the wetness, and inky stone-hewn chimneys reared indomitably through the hurling rain.

'And here's our housekeeper, Janet, to welcome us.' Blake sprang down and helped Emma as she rather awkwardly slithered to the ground. 'Janet, meet Emma, our new administrator.'

Emma approached the older lady with a smile. Janet stood on the top of the stone steps. Dressed in warm trousers and a jumper, her ample frame was covered by a flowered apron. Her grey hair was pulled back into a bun and her hands were folded in front of her.

'Welcome, my dear.' Janet stretched out her hand and took Emma's in a warm grip. 'Welcome to Leigh Manor. I'm sure you'll love it here. Now Blake — ' Her expression softened as she put a hand on his arm. ' — take Miss Marsden to her room, and I'll bring tea and biscuits into the dining room. I'm sure she must be cold and hungry after her journey.'

The housekeeper trotted away and Blake picked up Emma's case. 'Follow me,' he instructed, and led the way into the hall.

Paintings decked the walls and thick rugs covered the stained wood floor. A wooden staircase wound upwards into the shadows. As Emma followed Blake to her room, she was aware of warmth and comfort.

'The dining room is first on the right at the bottom of the stairs,' Blake said as he deposited her case on the floor. 'Perhaps you'd like to come down when you've settled in.'

The door shut behind her and Emma looked around. It was a large room, tastefully decorated in autumn colours. The carpet was thick beneath her toes, and she was pleasantly surprised to find a modern green-tiled bathroom behind a second door.

'Very luxurious,' she murmured to herself. 'As long as Mr Baron lives up to his surroundings, I might even enjoy this job.' She went to the tall window and was pleased to see the rain had eased a little. Her view arched over the back of the manor. Beyond the pebbled yard, she could see vegetable gardens stretching to a hedge. Beyond that she could see fields and woods, the trees stark in the winter gloom. To the right, building paraphernalia surrounded a mass of wooden and stone buildings.

Having finished her unpacking, she

ventured downstairs and found Blake waiting in the dining room. He was pouring tea. 'A log fire,' she exclaimed. 'How lovely.'

Revived by the tea and biscuits, she followed Blake to the office. It was obviously newly converted and held modern computers and equipment. 'Very nice,' she murmured as she noted the almost empty filing cabinets.

'Alex never does anything by halves,' Blake said lightly. 'If we're to diversify and make Leigh Manor thrive, then he'll want the tools for that to be the best.'

Emma nodded. The more she heard about Alex Baron, the more she was inclined to be impressed.

'My desk is over there.' Blake pointed to the other half of the room. 'I manage the day-to-day running of the farm, and the new investments of course. I live in the converted granary, so I'm available twenty-four hours a day.' He laughed.

Emma nodded. 'It all sounds well-organised,' she commented.

'Alex is always well-organised,' Blake agreed drily, and Emma glanced at him. Had she noticed an edge to his voice again? But he was smiling at her in a benign fashion, and she thought she must have been mistaken.

'I think I'll go and freshen up before dinner, Blake, if that's all right with you.'

'Of course,' Blake said quickly. 'We can go through everything tomorrow. I suggest you have the morning to yourself, and then we'll start work at midday.'

Emma nodded in relief.

'Alex is expected back in the early afternoon, and believe me, you won't get much rest once he takes over!'

The telephone interrupted them. Blake picked it up as Emma idly opened the drawers of her desk.

'Natalie, my sweet,' Blake cooed into the phone. 'No, Alex is still away. He'll be back tomorrow, and yes, I'll tell him. How are you ... ?' The phone obviously went dead as Blake held it away from his ear.

'Natalie Lawrence,' he said to Emma.

'Her father owns most of the land around Leigh Manor. She's rather got her eye on Alex, I think.' He compressed his lips. 'Of course, a match between those two would make the largest acreage in the area.' He sighed.

'Are they engaged?' Emma was curious. The strident tones had sounded rather demanding.

Blake shook his head. 'Not from want of Natalie trying! But Alex won't be shackled that easily. She's a beautiful woman, though.' His eyes had a faraway look, and Emma wondered if he had a soft spot for Natalie himself. 'But no doubt the owner of Leigh Manor is a better catch than its manager.' His voice was bitter and Emma glanced at him sharply. But the smile was back on his face and his eyes were twinkling. 'I expect she'll give any man a heap of trouble!' He laughed. 'So it's as well I'm not in the frame. Now, do you want to disappear for a while and I'll see you at dinner?'

Emma nodded and returned to her

room. She made a quick call to Celia, her flatmate.

'What's the boss like, and the manor?' Celia had been intrigued by the thought of her friend working in a country manor house, but had been supportive of Emma's decision, for which Emma was grateful.

'I haven't met him yet.' Emma laughed. 'He's away on business, due back tomorrow. But there's rather a dishy farm manager.' She kept her voice light. An overwhelming feeling of homesickness assailed her and she clutched the phone. She would miss Celia. 'I'll tell you everything tomorrow night,' she promised. Slowly she closed her phone, shrugged off her misgivings and sought comfort in a hot shower.

Dinner was an excellent meal, but tiredness overtook Emma as she sipped her coffee. 'I think I'll have an early night, Blake.'

He rose as she left, and she was thankful to slip into a comfortable bed and pull the duvet up to her chin.

* * *

She slept immediately, and was awakened by a chink of sunlight piercing the curtains. It had stopped raining. Pushing the curtains aside, she felt her spirits leap at the brightness. Fully refreshed from the dreamless sleep, she went in search of breakfast. Coffee, cereal and toast were on the table in the dining room, so she helped herself. There was no sign of Blake. Perhaps now was a good time to get a breath of fresh air and explore her surroundings before settling down to work. Changing into a pair of jeans and walking boots, she set off.

She wandered around the yard and gardens and marvelled at the completed conversion of the café. It looked light and airy, its picture windows facing the distant Welsh hills. The gardens were beautifully laid out, if rather sodden; but by spring, when the shrubs and trees regained their foliage, she imagined the whole area would be delightful.

In the neat borders she could see clumps of snowdrops nodding in the breeze, and daffodil shoots promised a rich display for the March opening.

She ventured further down the lane. The sun was dappling the hills and the rain glistened from the fir trees that lined the route. She leaned on a gate and looked across a meadow. At the far end a river twinkled in the sunlight.

On impulse, Emma opened the gate and walked through the grass. It really was lovely. Water gushed over stones and rocks, carrying twigs and leaves in its flow. She heard birds singing in the trees above her head and she felt a great peace wash over her. Suddenly she heard the sound of heavy breathing behind her. Startled, she turned round and found herself staring into the unblinking eyes of a bull.

'Oh my God!' Emma stood stock still in fright. Where on earth had this great beast come from?

She started to edge away from the river and slowly inched her way across the grass. The bull followed, his eyes never leaving her face. Emma knew she mustn't turn her back and run. She'd been told that as a child; she could hear her uncle's voice: 'If you run, the bull will run after you. Don't move suddenly, and don't make him angry.'

How do you tell if a bull is angry? Emma thought inconsequentially. It seemed a long way to the gate, and she shivered. 'One step at a time,' she muttered under her breath, and tried to breathe slowly. 'Keep calm; he won't hurt you.'

She edged gently backwards, but the bull showed no sign of leaving her alone. Every step Emma took, the bull edged closer. She was almost there. Then he lowered his nose and snorted, pawing the ground. The noise was terrifying. Emma gave a squeal and stopped moving.

She caught her breath as she heard a voice: 'There, there, Jumbo. It's all right.'

Emma didn't move. She felt a

presence behind her, and then a man was by her side. Tall and broad, he towered above her, his dark hair waving to his collar. He was ignoring her completely.

'Now Jumbo . . . ' He bent down and wrenched a handful of lush grass from under his feet. 'What have I here? Just for you.' He was stroking the great beast between his eyes as Emma watched, fascinated. The bull snuffled his hand noisily.

'Walk slowly to the gate,' the man ordered Emma, his voice cold. 'No sudden movements, just a gentle walk.'

Emma found that her legs were shaking as she obeyed, and slipped thankfully through the gate onto the road. The man followed, leaving Jumbo slavering.

'Now . . . ' The man turned his gaze onto Emma, and she felt herself shrivel beneath the contempt in his black eyes. 'What the hell did you think you were doing?'

'I'm sorry.' Emma felt tears prick her

eyes. 'I was going for a walk. I didn't know there was a bull in the field.'

'You damned tourists. Don't you know the law of trespass? There might be rights of way over my land, but this field is not one of them!'

Emma's fear turned to anger. Who on earth did he think he was? 'I'm sorry if I've trespassed,' she answered, her eyes flashing. 'But how was I to know there was a bull in that field? I don't see a sign!'

Green eyes glared into black and sparks raced across the air between them. For a second the man was silent, and then he turned towards his car, which was parked on the verge, and zapped the locks open.

'May I suggest you return to the village and purchase a map from the post office.' His voice was icy. 'Maybe then you'll keep to the appropriate paths and save wasting my precious time and upsetting my prize bull.'

'Upsetting your *bull*!' Emma's words were lost as he revved up the BMW and headed off up the lane in the direction of — Leigh Manor.

It was then Emma realised the enormity of her actions. 'Oh my goodness,' she whispered, her rescuer's words echoing in her head: *my land, my bull*. 'Oh my goodness!' she repeated, staring after the vehicle in horror. 'That was Alex Baron!'

2

Wearily, Emma trudged back towards Leigh Manor. What an introduction to her boss! Well, she thought as she squared her shoulders resolutely, all she could do was apologise and hope Alex Baron was the sort of man who was more interested in his business than in the behaviour of its administrator.

* * *

In the office, Blake was greeting Alex enthusiastically. 'Alex! We didn't expect you back until this afternoon.'

'The meeting finished sooner than expected.' Alex was frowning. 'I'd have been back half an hour earlier if it hadn't been for some dratted tourist in Jumbo's field!'

'In Jumbo's field?' Blake repeated, astonished. 'In this weather?'

'You'd think walkers could at least follow the maps. All my rights of way are clearly signposted — I've even removed hedges to put up stiles, and now I'm thinking of opening the gardens and grounds to the public. What more can I do?' Alex ran his fingers through his hair in exasperation.

Blake shrugged.

'I pulled into the lane and there she was, standing in the field with Jumbo almost sniffing at her nose!'

'So you rescued her?' Blake grinned.

'What else could I do? I gave Jumbo a titbit and told the woman to get out of the field. I'm afraid I gave her a piece of my mind.'

'As usual,' Blake remarked drily. 'But Jumbo wouldn't hurt a fly. He's the softest bull I've ever come across. He'd just be curious and want to make friends.'

'She didn't know that.' Alex grinned suddenly. 'I just hope she may have learned a lesson and will use maps in future. Anyway,' he sighed, sitting at his desk, 'how are things going? Has Miss Marsden arrived?'

'Emma? Yes, she's here. I told her to take the morning off, but I'm sure she'll be happy to start work straight away. I'll ask Janet if she's seen her.'

'Leave it for a while. I'm dying for a cuppa and I need to freshen up. It's a long drive. Let's say we'll meet at eleven.'

'Fine.' Blake rose. 'It's good to have you back, old boy.'

Alex grinned at him affectionately.

At that moment there was a knock on the door and it was pushed slowly open.

★   ★   ★

Emma had crept quietly to her room on her return and had changed into a severe suit and blouse. Curbing her unruly curls, she hoped she now presented a professional appearance. Best to take the bull by the horns. She smiled to herself at the comparison and

22

made her way to the office. The meeting with Alex Baron couldn't be postponed any longer and she wanted to get it over with.

Blake went towards her as she stepped into the room. 'Ah, Emma. We were just talking about you. Come and meet Alex. He's returned earlier than expected.' He turned to Alex, beaming. But his boss's face was a picture of disbelief and anger.

'You!' He glared at Emma.

'Good morning, Mr Baron.' Emma tried to keep her voice steady.

'You've met?' Blake looked from one to another in astonishment.

Emma nodded. 'Unfortunately, yes.' She smiled tentatively. 'And I apologise for that first encounter. It was foolish of me and I hope you'll forgive me.' There, she had apologised. Now it was up to Alex.

'Foolish?' he said angrily. 'Do you mean to say — ' He turned to Blake. ' — this is my new secretary?'

Blake started to laugh. 'So this is

your errant tourist, Alex. Well I never.' Blake couldn't contain his laughter and Emma felt the colour rise in her face. Alex was still looking thunderous, and she realised she was probably about to lose her job before she had even started!

Alex ran his fingers through his hair and took a deep breath. Turning to Emma, he surveyed her from head to foot. She felt her anger rising. She had apologised; surely that was enough? She didn't like the way his cold gaze was sweeping over her and she shuddered. Mr Baron, the owner of Leigh Manor, gave the impression of a rude, arrogant landowner. She wasn't sure she wanted to stay anyway! Angrily, she lifted her eyes and returned his glare. For a moment their gazes locked, and then he turned away.

'I'll just go and freshen up, Blake. We'll meet in half an hour, Miss Marsden.' He looked at her coldly. 'Perhaps we can run through the work schedule before lunch.'

'Of course, Mr Baron,' she replied haughtily. 'That's what I'm here for.'

Deliberately, she turned away and switched on her computer, concentrating on the screen. She didn't look up as he left the room, but she breathed a sigh of relief. It looked as if she might be staying after all, though she didn't think working with Alex Baron was going to be very pleasant.

Blake was still chuckling, and Emma glared at him. 'Don't mind Alex,' he said, a grin on his face. 'I'm afraid he thinks more of his cattle than he does of women.'

Emma raised her eyebrows.

'Not your fault,' he tried to mollify her. 'He has little respect for the fairer sex at any time, and if you upset Jumbo . . . '

'Jumbo upset me,' Emma replied hotly. 'And I can't help it if Alex doesn't like women.'

'No, you can't.' Blake's voice was thoughtful. 'I'm afraid that's the way Alex is.' He hesitated as if to say more;

then, thinking better of it, he left the room.

Emma's thoughts whirled in turmoil, and she tried to calm herself as she waited nervously for the appearance of her employer. He arrived and pulled up a chair next to her.

'Now,' he began, leaning towards the screen, 'let's go through the details.'

Emma took a deep breath and made copious notes as Alex outlined the new outlets at Leigh Manor. It all sounded extremely professional and competent.

Finally Alex leaned back. 'Does it all make sense?' He looked at her quizzically for a moment. 'Miss Frobisher seemed to think you were ideal for the position. I do hope I can trust her judgment.'

'I've never had any complaints about my work before,' Emma said quietly.

'Then I'm sure I can count on you,' Alex answered smoothly, his cool gaze disconcerting. 'I want someone immediately, so I don't have time to reconsider. Shall we say a month's trial and then reassess the situation?' He rose without waiting for a reply.

'That will suit me,' Emma replied.

'Then I'll leave Blake to fill you in on anything else you need to know. There's some paperwork that needs sorting.' He waved towards a bulging in-tray. 'I'll let you get on with it.'

Alex looked at her for a moment. His eyes were unfathomable, and Emma squirmed under the dark gaze. 'I'll see you at lunch,' he said abruptly.

Emma breathed a sigh of relief as he left the office.

★ ★ ★

Lunch was a quiet meal, the atmosphere full of tension. Alex and Blake discussed Leigh Manor and, although Blake tried to include Emma in the conversation, Alex was cool in his comments to her.

'I see the barns are nearly finished,' he said.

'They'll be ready to move into next

week,' Blake confirmed. 'I've spoken to the one fellow who's interested. He's an agent for several artists and seems very keen.'

'He'll come and inspect the building?'

Blake nodded. 'He's got a client lined up as a potential working artist, and then there'll be a gallery area.'

'And we get a cut of the takings?'

'Plus rent and utility expenses, of course.'

'Sounds like a good deal to me.'

'If we can get the other barn finished as well, that will divide up, and I thought maybe the potter from the village,' Blake said enthusiastically. 'I know he's looking for somewhere to build a new wheel, and he'll have a display area as well. Tourists love to see us ruralites working!'

'Approach whoever you think is suitable, Blake. I'll leave that in your hands. As long as everything's up and running in the next two weeks. That leaves us one week to sort out any hitches. The opening is the following Saturday, and I've invited the press as well as local dignitaries. We want to make a big splash with plenty of publicity.' He turned to Emma. 'I have a couple of phone calls to make, so we'll meet in the office at two.'

★　★　★

That afternoon, Alex's mood was a complete contrast. 'Emma, I'd like to apologise for my earlier bad temper,' he said. 'I'd had a difficult journey, and the sight of you in Jumbo's field was the last straw. I overreacted, of course.'

'You did.' Emma wasn't sure how to handle this charming Alex.

'Anyway, now we have to work together, and I want the business running smoothly from the outset, so perhaps we can forget our unfortunate meeting and start again?'

Emma looked at him. He was smiling warmly and there was a twinkle in the black eyes. For a long moment their eyes met and locked, and she felt the same surge of feeling sweep through her as she had on their first encounter. This man was dangerous! Arrogant, rude and charming — a lethal combination; and she had no intention of ever becoming involved with a charming man again. However, as he said, they had to work together; and if things became too unpleasant, she could always return to London and Tony Merriman.

'Of course, Alex,' she answered, and pulled her gaze away.

The afternoon passed surprisingly pleasantly, and Emma found herself enjoying the work. The details of Leigh Leisure had been carefully recorded, each project having its own accounts and reports so that progress could be monitored. Emma relaxed as she explored the well-organised business.

'I think we'll call it a day, Emma,' Alex said at last, and she straightened her back. 'I'm sure you'd like to freshen up before dinner. Shall we meet in the dining room at seven o'clock?'

Emma nodded and watched him leave the room. He was a very attractive man, she had to admit, and she had enjoyed working with him. He had a good financial mind and his business ideas were creative and exciting. Pensively, she closed down the computer and returned to her room. She flopped down on the bed and, reaching for her mobile, she dialled home.

Celia answered immediately. 'Emma, how's it going?'

'Well . . . ' Emma hesitated. 'I'm still here.'

'I should hope so, too — you only left yesterday! What's the matter?'

Emma heard the alarm in Celia's voice and hastened to explain. As she detailed her first encounter with Alex, Celia burst into peals of laughter.

'Oh, Emma, a bull? What rotten luck. But Alex — what's he really like?'

'I'm not sure,' Emma replied thoughtfully. 'He seems to have forgiven my trespassing on his land, and this afternoon he was charming . . . '

'But?' Celia sensed the reserve in Emma's voice.

'Well, first impressions count, and I found him arrogant and rude.'

'Oh!' Celia was startled. 'Perhaps he thought you meant some harm to Jumbo?'

'Me, harm Jumbo?' Emma laughed. 'You should see the size of him, Celia. No. Alex did apologise, though; said he was tired after the journey. And I couldn't fault his manner all afternoon.'

'I still hear a big 'but',' Celia said.

'But I'm sure things will work out,' Emma answered quickly. 'Leigh Manor is lovely and the projects are exciting. I can see this being a very interesting job, for a while anyway.'

'Well, don't get too settled. I miss you already.'

'I don't think there's much chance of that,' Emma promised. 'But I'll be home for a weekend as soon as I see how the work schedule goes. Then I can tell you all the gory details of Leigh Manor.'

'And Alex,' Celia added with a smile as she rang off and stared at the phone thoughtfully for a moment.

She hadn't heard her friend so rattled about a man since . . . Sighing, she went to the kitchen. Emma had gone to Herefordshire to regain her equilibrium, though after that phone call, Celia wasn't sure she had made the right choice. Oh well, she thought to herself as she filled the kettle, time would tell.

Emma was also wondering at her decision to run away from London. Had it really been necessary? Feeling forlorn, she heaved herself off the bed and headed for the bathroom. Taking a shower, she dressed in a soft green wool dress that accentuated the auburn curls that she smoothed with her brush. With a final glance in the mirror, she went down to dinner. Blake was already in the dining room and offered her a glass of wine. Smiling, she took it.

'I've just got to make a phone call,' he said. 'Shan't be a moment.'

Emma wandered round the room, taking in the view of the gardens from the bay window. Even in winter they were beautiful.

At that moment the door swung open and a stunning blond entered the room. Emma had time to notice a sleek silk suit and cloying perfume before the woman stopped in front of her.

'Who are you?' Her voice was haughty and she glared at Emma suspiciously.

'I'm Emma Marsden,' she replied quietly. 'Who are you?'

The woman glared at her. 'I'm Natalie Lawrence,' she replied, her glance sweeping Emma from head to toe. 'Alex's fiancée. Where is he?'

'I haven't the faintest idea,' Emma said. 'I'm sure he's around somewhere.'

'So you're his new PA?' Diane's voice was assessing. 'From London?' Emma nodded and Diane's eyes narrowed. 'What made you come to Hereford-shire?'

'I needed a change,' Emma answered,

and Diane's eyebrows lifted.

'I see.' Diane's voice was cold, but she obviously didn't 'see' and continued to stare at Emma who, feeling distinctly uncomfortable, returned her gaze to the darkening view.

There was a stony silence, and then Emma heard the angry click of heels as Diane left the room and slammed the door. Emma smiled grimly to herself. So that was the beautiful Diane that both men admired. Well, she had met better-tempered women in her time. She sighed and sipped her wine.

'Did I see Diane in the hall?' Blake asked as he returned.

Emma nodded. 'She was looking for Alex. I thought you said they weren't engaged?'

'I did!' Blake looked startled.

'Well, she introduced herself as Alex's fiancée,' Emma replied drily.

'Oh.' For a moment Blake looked angry, then he grinned. 'I doubt Alex is aware of that fact. I'm sure he would've told me if there'd been an engagement.'

'You've known Alex a long time?' Emma was curious.

Blake nodded. 'We were at Oxford together, became close friends, and . . .' He stopped suddenly as Janet entered. 'Ah.' He sounded relieved. 'Dinner is ready, I believe.'

Alex was late arriving at the table and his expression was forbidding. There was no sign of Diane; she had obviously not been invited to dine with them.

* * *

The next few days passed quickly and Emma settled into a routine. The work was interesting, and she found herself becoming absorbed in Leigh Manor and its projects. She saw little of Alex as he strode around the grounds and buildings, checking on work done as the day of completion loomed near.

It was early in the morning, as she and Blake worked in companionable silence, that there was a knock on the door.

Blake jumped up. 'That will be the agent. He said he'd come this week. We're hoping to get the artist installed next week.'

He opened the door with a flourish and ushered in a smartly dressed businessman, with blond waves and blue eyes that twinkled in his handsome face. A man that oozed charm; a dangerous man.

Emma sat rooted to her seat, eyes enormous in her white face, and her heart beat frantically as she tried to swallow her shock.

'Emma,' Blake said as he ushered the man forward, 'meet Frank Lander.'

'Well, well . . . ' Frank Lander's eyes narrowed. 'If it isn't my Emma. Fancy finding you here!'

3

At that moment Alex entered the office.

'Alex,' Blake said, looking relieved at the interruption, 'this is Frank Lander. He's come to inspect the gallery. Hopefully we'll have an artist installed next Monday.' He shot a pleading look at Emma.

'Mr Lander.' Alex smiled and held out his hand. 'How do you do?'

'Frank, please.' The two men shook hands, and Emma tried desperately to gather her scattered wits.

'It'll be a pleasure doing business with you, I'm sure.' Alex was being charming to the prospective investor. 'Blake's run through all the details with you?'

'Everything's agreed.' Blake laughed jovially. 'The contract is ready to sign. Frank just wants to see the venue.'

'Of course.' Alex smiled. 'Emma,

could you arrange coffee please, and then we'll take Frank on a tour of inspection.'

Emma got to her feet and found she was shaking. 'Coffee. Of course.' Her voice was husky. 'Still black with two sugars, Frank?' The sarcasm was evident in her voice, and Alex frowned.

'You two know one another?'

'You could say that!' Emma shot a venomous look at Frank.

'Let's just say we're old friends.' Frank's voice was soft, but his eyes glinted. 'I'm sure our friendship won't interfere with our business arrangements.' He raised an eyebrow pointedly at Emma.

She didn't comment and left to fetch coffee, but inside she was fuming. Handing out the cups, she refused to meet Frank's gaze, and didn't utter another word as the men left to see the buildings.

She tried to concentrate on her work, but it was difficult; and when Alex marched into the office an hour later, she was unprepared for his anger.

'What on earth possessed you to be so rude?' he demanded, leaning over her desk. 'Our first potential investor, and you try to sabotage the whole thing?' He ran his fingers through his hair and paced the room. 'I gave you the benefit of the doubt after your first irrational display of behaviour, but now I'm beginning to wonder. If you treat all our investors like that, we'll be bankrupt before we begin!' He glared at her. 'Well, Emma, I'm waiting for an explanation!'

'Has Frank pulled out?' Emma's voice wobbled.

'No, but it's no thanks to you! I gather you and he had some sort of relationship in London, and when he finished it, you took it badly. Obsessive jealousy, he called it.'

'Obsessive jealousy?' Emma's anger ignited. 'Frank said I was jealous?' Her voice was incredulous.

'And weren't you?'

'Of course I was jealous!' Her temper

flared. 'So would you have been in my circumstances.'

'Emma, I'm really not interested in your private life.' Alex held up his hand, his dark eyes flashing. 'What I *am* interested in is your behaviour as my secretary. And that, this morning, was appalling.'

So he was judging her by what Frank had told him. Emma bit her lip to restrain further retort. If he wanted to believe Frank, fine. Why should she care? And if Frank was going to be visiting Leigh Manor, then it would probably be as well if she left. After all, it was Frank's fault she had applied for this job in the first place. She had been trying to escape him, and now he had followed her here. Perhaps he had got her address from Miss Frobisher — though Emma had to admit it was unlikely. Besides, Blake had set up this agreement with Frank before she had even arrived. Frank was always looking for new investments, and somehow he and Blake had met and come to an arrangement. No, it was all one horrible coincidence.

She stared at Alex and wondered what to say. 'I'm sorry,' she said at last. 'I shouldn't have reacted as I did. But it was a shock seeing Frank here, and I couldn't think straight.'

'Obviously!' Alex glared at her. 'Perhaps in future you might try to keep your emotions in check when important people walk through that door.'

'So I'm not fired?'

Alex sighed. 'I don't have time to run around looking for another secretary at the moment. But I warn you, one more outburst like that and you'll be back on the first train to London.'

'Thank you,' Emma said demurely. 'I promise to speak to Frank politely in future.'

'There shouldn't be any need.' He looked at her sharply. 'He's signing the contract now. Blake thought he ought to finish the business elsewhere in the circumstances. I doubt Frank will be visiting too often once the artist is installed. Blake will let you have all the details for the records.' He stared at her for a moment, his face perplexed. 'I really don't understand you, Emma. But then, women are beyond any man's comprehension!' And with that sweeping statement, he left the office, slamming the door behind him.

Emma heaved a sigh of relief. At least she still had her job. But the thought of Frank Lander appearing in the future left her with a heavy heart. Taking a deep breath, she headed for the kitchen. She needed a coffee before she started again, and a few minutes' break would calm her nerves.

Janet was rolling pastry on the scrubbed wooden table. The kitchen was a pleasant room, large and airy, with windows stretching the length of the back wall. A delicious smell of baking filled the air, and Janet's face was pink from cooking.

She looked up as Emma filled the kettle and fetched a mug. 'Alex upsetting you?' she asked shrewdly. 'I heard raised voices.'

Emma smiled rather crookedly. 'It seems to be me upsetting Alex,' she replied. 'I can't do anything right. I've always been so competent before, and I've done more difficult jobs than this. Yet here, I always seem to show myself up as an idiot! Coffee, Janet?'

Janet nodded and wrapped the pastry carefully around the rolling pin to lay it on the plate. 'Alex can be difficult,' she demurred. 'He's not had much to do with women. Blake has always done his office work, with the help of young Patti from the village when they were busy.'

'But he must have had girlfriends. What about Diane?' Emma sat on one of the stools, watching Janet's deft fingers slicing apple into the pie case.

'Ah, that one!' Janet's voice held derision. 'She's no good for him, that one. Out for all she can get. Sees Alex as her key to owning more acres, and he's attractive as well.'

Emma smiled. 'I imagine Diane usually gets what she wants.'

'Not Alex, she won't. Used to go around with Blake before Alex came on the scene. Blake introduced them and she spotted a better catch.'

'Have you known them long?'

'Blake, all his life. He's . . . ' Janet hesitated. 'He's a local lad. I used to look after him when he was a babe. His mum worked part-time, God rest her soul. I got to know Alex when he was studying with Blake. Used to have holidays in Kestleigh regular together. Right chums, they were.'

Emma looked thoughtful. 'They're not much alike.'

Janet shook her head and her face softened. 'Blake was always a charmer. A smiler, I used to call him when he was tiny — loved life and everyone.' She sighed. 'He just hadn't got much business sense. Alex has taught him all he knows, and Blake's good at his job,' she added defensively.

'I'm sure,' Emma murmured. 'But Alex?' she persisted.

'Alex's mum left him when he was a

small lad. His dad was a financier, very wrapped up in his job. I think Alex missed female loving. Never got over his mum going away. Don't mention it to him, mind; very sore subject.'

'I shan't,' Emma said. She didn't want to mention anything that would upset Alex again.

'Never seemed to settle with a girlfriend,' Janet added. 'I don't think he likes women very much.'

Emma had to agree with that sentiment; and as she made her way back to the office, she pondered on Janet's words. Certainly, they explained his attitude and his short temper. It was a pity, Emma thought as she switched on her computer. Alex was most women's dream: handsome, well-off and intelligent. But like a bear with a sore head most of the time! She smiled wryly and started on the paperwork.

Later that day, Alex and Blake walked into the office. 'Now,' Alex said as he made notes on a pad, 'can I ask you to stay at Leigh Manor the next couple of weekends, Emma? The open day is on the following Saturday, and I could do with all the help I can get.'

'Of course,' Emma answered immediately, shelving her plans to return to London.

'And you'll be here, Blake?'

'Wouldn't miss it for the world,' Blake answered cheerfully.

'Everything will be in order?' Alex was checking a list.

Blake nodded. 'The artist, a woman by the name of Josephine, is arriving with her equipment on Monday. She's also bringing a stock of paintings for the gallery. Tom from the village is supervising the pottery shed, and he should be ready. Then there's Eric and Patti, who are opening the workshop and displaying their wood carvings.'

'Patti who helps out here occasionally?'

'Her husband's a wood carver; candlesticks and so on. He's very good. And she does crochet work. They'll make an interesting attraction.'

'The café? Gift shop?'

'All completed, furbished and staffed. Ready to go.' Blake grinned.

'You have been busy!'

'Of course. You were away in London for a month, don't forget.' Blake's voice had a slight edge. 'Things moved fast once the initial building was complete.'

'All right!' Alex held up his hand and grinned affectionately at Blake. 'I realise how hard you've been working while I've been swanning around the city. I've done several tours of inspection, and your work is appreciated. I'm just confirming that there are no problems. I want to make a grand splash on open day.'

'You'll make that all right,' Blake agreed. You'll have the whole of Kestleigh here for a start. They're agog to see what you've accomplished.'

'We've accomplished, Blake,' Alex corrected. 'I couldn't have done it without you.'

Blake looked pleased, and Alex turned his attention to his secretary.

'Now, Emma . . . ' She felt her stomach squirm under the intensity of his dark gaze. 'Diane will be acting as hostess, and your duty will be to mingle with the guests, answer any questions, and generally tell everyone what a success the venture is going to be!' He smiled, and she felt herself glow with pleasure.

The glow was short-lived as he frowned suddenly. 'Frank Lander will be here, so I expect you to apologise and treat him with respect. And there will be several possible investors, people I've persuaded to visit from London. Some will be our guests for the weekend. Please,' he added as he leaned forward, 'if you recognise any of these guests, try and restrain any negative reactions.'

Emma bristled. 'I'm sure I shan't know any of them,' she replied stiffly. 'And as for Frank, of course I'll treat him politely, as I will any other guest. I want this to be a success, as well you know.' She glared at him, green sparks flying.

'Hmm.' He leaned back. 'I'll take your word for it.'

The afternoon passed in a haze of activity, and Emma felt her excitement mounting. The project at Leigh Manor was exhilarating, and she always gave her best under pressure. She was really looking forward to the opening.

★　★　★

The next days saw vans unloading, strangers dashing around, and a thrilling air of bustle pervading the scene. Alex seemed to be everywhere at once, and even Blake was rushing around. Emma's fingers flew over the keyboard, the telephone remained almost permanently in her left hand, and Janet was tutting over the temporary staff engaged to help her with the catering.

For the first time since she had left Tony Merriman's employ, Emma felt the adrenalin flow and the buzz whiz through her brain. This was more like it! She grinned happily to herself as she watched the organised chaos.

The day of the opening dawned bright and clear, and breakfast was early. Emma entered the room, and even Alex's eyes showed admiration as he carefully surveyed her. She had worn a honey-coloured dress that accentuated her figure and emphasised the rich auburn of her hair.

'Wow!' Blake grinned mischievously. 'You'll certainly encourage interest in that outfit.'

Alex passed her the coffee pot. 'You look very nice, Emma,' he commented quietly, and Emma suppressed a smile. A compliment from Alex was worth recording.

Alex sped through the details of the day as they ate. He said nothing that they didn't already know by heart, and Emma was surprised to note the tension in his voice. Of course, this was the culmination of years of work; and from what she had seen in the accounts, he had invested a large sum in the venture. A lot of people stood to lose, should Leigh Leisure fail. She knew from working with Tony how a venture could suddenly founder for no apparent reason, and her stomach churned. Today meant so much.

Diane arrived as they were finishing. Looking rather exotic in a silk dress and coat of various hues of orange, she looked every inch the wealthy hostess. Her sweeping gaze took in Emma's simple dress and dismissed it with a satisfied smile. She turned to Alex. 'Right, Alex darling.' She slipped a hand through his arm. 'Lead on. The gates are about to open.'

A fleeting frown creased his brow, and then he led the way outside. Emma had to admit that Alex and Diane made a striking pair, but she dismissed the dismal thought and concentrated on the throng that was waiting at the gates.

The hours passed quickly. Guests were introduced, wine glasses were filled, and conversation buzzed. The sun shone, and at lunchtime Emma managed to slip away to the kitchen in the hope of a quick coffee. Alex was already there, his expression taut but happy.

'It's going wonderfully, I think,' Emma said as she helped herself to a drink. 'Everyone seems very impressed.'

'I heard you talking to Mike Talbot,' Alex said abruptly, and Emma's heart dropped. 'You were brilliant.'

She almost spilled her coffee as she stared at him.

'You sounded as if you knew what you were talking about, and business-wise, you made an excellent impression.'

'I did?'

Alex nodded. 'Mike came to see me afterwards. He's thinking of recommending an investment from one of his colleagues. He's got some very influential contacts.'

'That's wonderful,' Emma murmured.

'Perhaps you'll make a useful addition to the team after all.' He smiled at her and placed his mug on the table. 'Must dash now, but well done, Emma.' He touched her briefly on the arm and her skin tingled. She watched the door close and stood stupefied, clutching her mug. Praise from Alex was praise indeed! Shaking herself free from her stupor, she smiled to herself and her heart somersaulted. At last she was making the right impression. Humming, she returned to the fray.

She had managed to avoid Frank Lander for most of the day. When their paths did cross, she greeted him with a polite smile and moved away. She checked the guests who were staying and was relieved to find he was not one of them.

She and Alex passed each other several times that afternoon, and each time she was rewarded with a smile. On their last encounter, he introduced her to an interested gentleman with the words, 'I'll leave you in the capable hands of my assistant, Emma Marsden. She'll give you all the financial information you need.' Her heart swelled with pride.

It was early evening before the last

stragglers wandered out through the wrought-iron gates. Those staying had returned to their rooms to change for dinner, and Emma slipped into the office to make a few notes before she went upstairs. She was exhausted, but exhilarated. The day had undoubtedly been a success; and as the door opened, she turned with a smile. Her smile faded as she faced Frank Lander.

'Did you want something, Frank?' She kept her voice cool, but tension gripped her stomach.

'I've hardly seen you all day, Emma.' His voice was peeved and his eyes were like cold steel as they sliced into hers. 'I thought we might have a little chat.'

'There's nothing to talk about, Frank.' Emma started towards the door, but Frank closed it and barred her way. She stood still.

'I think there is, Emma.' He moved slowly towards her. 'I've missed you.'

'Frank,' Emma said as she brushed her hand across her forehead wearily, 'I've nothing further to say to you. It's over. I don't want to see you again, and I'm really very tired. If you don't mind, I'd like to go to my room and freshen up for dinner.'

'Oh, but I do mind!' He was smiling in a way that sent shivers down Emma's spine. She backed away as he approached, and then she felt the hard wood of her desk against her spine. Trying to keep her breathing even, she faced him, her eyes sparking with anger.

'Get out of my way, Frank!' She leaned forward and pushed him with all her force, sidestepping and heading for the door. But he was too quick for her and caught her arm.

'Not so fast.' His face was close to hers. 'We haven't finished yet!'

He was strong — she remembered that; and, despite her struggles, he locked her in an embrace. She squirmed to avoid his hot breath as he bent to kiss her.

'Let me go,' she hissed, and brought her foot up to kick him squarely on the shin with her pointed toes.

'You bitch!' he yelped, and his fingers dug into her arms.

'Miss Marsden!' The voice was ice-cold, and Emma felt the grip on her arms loosen. Pulling herself free, she caught her breath at the fury on Alex's face.

'Just a little disagreement between old friends.' Frank was grinning and straightening his tie. 'Don't worry, Alex, Emma was just reminding me of her attractive charms.'

'I was . . . what?' Emma was speechless. She was shaking with shock and anger, and the smug expression on Frank's face made her realise he had neatly turned everything into her fault again. 'You attacked me!'

'Come, come, sweetheart. I'd hardly say that.' Frank laughed and turned towards Alex. 'Women, eh, Alex? Well, I must be on my way. I've a long journey back to London. Sorry to disappoint you, my lovely.' His eyes were cold as he smiled at Emma. 'Perhaps another time.' And he had gone, closing the door gently behind him.

'Alex . . . ' Emma tried to regain her composure.

'I suggest you go and tidy yourself for dinner, Emma.' Alex's tone was sarcastic. 'I shall expect you in the dining room in half an hour. And please, if at all possible, try to act in a suitable manner. We'll talk about this incident another time.'

He swung on his heel and left the room. The door slammed and Emma sank onto her chair, the tears spilling over.

4

Taking a deep breath, Emma got shakily to her feet and sped to her room. Thankfully, she encountered no one along the way. Washing her face, she reapplied her makeup and then dressed in a lightweight beige suit. Her reflection in the mirror showed an efficient secretary; it was only her haunted eyes that belied her calm.

Alex handed her a glass of wine as she entered. The conversation buzzed around her, and fearfully she met his gaze.

'Are you all right?' His voice was abrupt and his eyes were unfathomable. Emma nodded. 'Yes, thank you.' She managed a bright smile, but her hand shook slightly as she sipped the wine. 'It wasn't my fault you know,' she said quietly.

He looked at her for a moment in

silence. 'We'll talk about it in the morning.' He turned away and approached one of the guests, leaving her to sip her fortifying wine.

Dinner was an ordeal. Already tired, and in turmoil after the encounter with Frank, Emma longed for bed. After what seemed like an eternity, she finally managed to escape; and as her head touched the soft down of her pillow, her last thoughts were of Alex.

★   ★   ★

She awoke, amazed to find she had slept the night through. Feeling better as the sun streamed through the window, her optimism returned; and despite the forthcoming interview with Alex, she went down to breakfast feeling determinedly cheerful.

The office seemed quiet after the bustle of the opening day. Emma thought maybe she wasn't expected in early on a Sunday, but she couldn't settle to anything else, and the thought of exploring conjured up pictures of Jumbo. Besides, she was tired.

Concentrating on some routine correspondence, she looked up warily as the door opened. It was Blake.

'Morning, Emma,' he said cheerfully. 'I didn't expect to see you here. I thought you'd be resting after the hectic day yesterday.'

She grinned. 'I know. I thought I'd tidy up a few letters, that's all. How are you this morning?'

'Wonderful.' He rubbed his hands together. 'Yesterday was really fantastic. It all went extremely well, I think.'

Emma nodded. 'With any luck there'll be a good write-up in the press, and I noticed that one of the tourism magazines was represented. We should get our share of visitors for the rest of the summer.'

'Hopefully,' Blake agreed. 'I think Alex wants to open on Sundays from next weekend. Sunday is traditionally a 'day out' around these parts, so we want to catch the day trippers as well.'

'I'm sure it'll be a success. Everyone was raring to start working properly now that the workshops are officially open.'

At that point, the door opened again and Alex walked in. Emma felt her heart somersault; now for a lecture. But he was smiling.

'Here you are. I did wonder if you might be resting. It's Sunday, and we are closed, you know.'

'No way,' Blake said enthusiastically. 'Let's get the show on the road! There are still things to do.'

'Not that much,' Alex replied. 'Anything important can wait until Monday. I've given Janet the day off; she deserves it after all her hard work yesterday. And I thought I might take the rest of the staff out to dinner this evening, to celebrate the opening.'

'Sounds grand.' Blake seemed delighted, but Emma looked at Alex guardedly.

'I've booked a table for four at The Jolly Duck,' Alex continued. 'The three of us, and Diane of course. She made an impressive hostess.'

'That'll be great.' Blake yawned suddenly and stretched his arms. 'I think I'll go and rustle up some coffee, then we can go through any points raised from yesterday.'

'Good idea,' Alex said smoothly. As the door closed behind Blake, Emma was aware of the cool eyes boring into her. 'Well, Emma?'

Emma cleared her throat and felt the colour rise in her cheeks. 'Alex, I'm sorry for the scene you witnessed, but believe me, it was not of my making.'

He raised an eyebrow and continued to gaze at her as he perched on the side of her desk.

'Frank and I were in a relationship, but it was me who finished it. I found him . . . ' She hesitated. ' . . . untrust-worthy. And I can't have a serious relationship with a man I don't trust.'

'And yesterday?' Alex was watching her, his expression inscrutable.

She sighed. 'Frank had been drinking wine.' She decided to be charitable.

After all, Frank was an investor in Leigh Manor. 'I think he just wanted to see if I still cared for him. I'm sure he'll be regretting it this morning.' She felt her colour deepen further under Alex's scrutiny and clenched her teeth. Why she should make excuses for Frank she had no idea, but she found herself wanting to stay at Leigh Manor, very much; and if Frank were to be part of Leigh Leisure, then she would just have to bury her dislike.

'Hmm.' Alex was fiddling with a paperclip as he listened. Then he sighed and stood up as they heard Blake approaching down the corridor. 'We'll let the matter drop now, Emma. It was such a successful day, and I don't want to mar our enjoyment of that fact. But please, can you try and concentrate on being the good administrator I know you can be?'

'Of course,' Emma replied smoothly, relief flooding through her.

'I can't fathom you at all, Emma.' Alex shook his head in bewilderment. 'I really can't. One minute you're every-thing I'm looking for in the project, and the next I wonder if the agency is out to sabotage me!'

'Oh, really!' Emma replied indig-nantly. She was forestalled from further comment by the entrance of Blake balancing a tray.

'Ah, Blake. Coffee. Excellent.' Alex beamed, and Emma's indignation sub-sided.

Let it go, she thought wryly. *Let it go, with all the other gaffs.*

* * *

The day passed pleasantly, and Emma returned to her room to dress for the evening out. Descending the stairs, she heard a low wolf whistle, and smiled down at a grinning Blake. She had tried her best and was wearing an elegant skirt of vibrant blue that swirled about her calves. Topped by a cream silk blouse with her hair brushed to a glowing cap, she did indeed look attractive. Diane raised an eyebrow as she swept into the hall in a long dress of amber satin that would have graced any ball. The men had donned their suits.

'My,' Blake said as he offered his arm to Emma, 'don't we look a grand party.'

Emma's spirits lifted as they entered The Jolly Duck. Despite its name, it looked extremely elegant, decorated in muted creams and rusts. The tables were alcoved and the chairs comfortable. Soft music echoed in the background, and even the bar had an air of quiet refinement.

Blake held out Emma's chair. 'What do you think, Emma?'

'Lovely.' Emma looked around in appreciation. 'This is really pleasing.'

Alex smiled. 'I'm glad you like it, Emma. We dine here quite often, when we have something to celebrate, or to entertain guests. They've never let us down yet.'

'There's dancing later.' Blake pointed to a wooden-floored square at the far end. 'They usually have a small combo and their music is excellent.'

The food proved to be as good as Alex had promised, and after the first initial feeling of awkwardness, Emma relaxed. The main topic of conversation was Leigh Manor. Although Diane wasn't rude to Emma, all her comments were directed at Alex and occasionally Blake. Emma remained quiet, enjoying the atmosphere and the delicious local beef that had been her choice of main dish. As coffee was served, she heard the notes of the combo tuning up. Couples started to leave their tables, and Diane stood up.

'Dance, Alex?'

Emma had to admit they were well-matched. Alex danced beautifully, and Diane fitted into his arms perfectly. Emma glanced across at Blake, and for a moment his jealousy was plain to see in his grim expression.

So she had been right: Blake still cared for Diane. She sighed. She was sure Diane wouldn't make any man particularly happy, least of all Blake with his fun-loving personality; but if Blake were in love with Diane, there was nothing she could do. And Diane was obviously favouring Alex. She wondered how Alex felt, and suddenly a feeling of loneliness overwhelmed her. Next weekend, she vowed, she would return home for a couple of days, meet her friends, and wash Leigh Manor out of her hair — and Alex with it!

No sooner had the couple returned than Blake was on his feet. 'My turn, Diane?' He held out his hand. Diane looked as if she were going to refuse and then shrugged.

'Of course, Blake.' She took his arm and they threaded their way through the tables.

'Emma?' Alex was still standing. 'Would you care to dance?'

For a moment she hesitated; and then, her heart fluttering, she smiled. 'Thank you, Alex, I'd love to.'

The music was soft as Alex's arm tightened round her, and their steps matched perfectly. She could feel his breath on her hair and for a moment she closed her eyes. All her instincts told her this was a bad idea, but her emotions told her otherwise — she was falling in love with Alex Baron. As the thought drifted through her relaxed mind, she opened her eyes with a start.

Diane was glaring at her over Blake's shoulder, and she grinned wryly to herself. Whatever she felt was a fantasy; there was no sense at all in falling in love with Alex. It would be even more disastrous than her love affair with Frank! Why was she such an idiot with men?

No, there was just one thing for it. She had to control her emotions and distance herself for a while; a long weekend away was definitely on the cards. She would ask Alex if he could release her for a few days. Then perhaps in London she could get her thoughts into perspective and return to reality.

The dance ended too quickly, and as their bodies lost contact Emma felt a chill. Alex was looking down at her with a strange expression in his black eyes, and she caught her breath.

'Thank you, Emma.' His voice was husky as he held her arm and guided her back to the table. 'That was delightful.'

Diane's eyes were venomous as she glared at Emma, but she kept a smile fixed on her lips. The relaxed atmosphere had departed, leaving tension around the table.

It wasn't long before they left and headed back to Leigh Manor. Diane was dropped off at her front door, much to her obvious chagrin.

'Thank you for a wonderful evening, Alex.' Emma smiled as she bade the men goodnight in the hall. 'It really was a delicious meal and I did enjoy it.'

Alex smiled. 'It did us all good, I think. Goodnight, Emma.'

The two men headed for the dining room for a nightcap, and Emma slipped gratefully into bed. As she drifted into sleep, the last thought in her mind was of gliding sweetly around the dance floor in Alex's arms to the strains of the 'Anniversary Waltz'.

★   ★   ★

When Alex entered the office the next day, Emma waited with bated breath. Would their dance have changed his attitude? She chided herself for her thoughts. Really, she was acting like a besotted teenager!

In fact, other than bidding her a cool 'good morning', Alex practically ignored her. She smiled wryly to herself and eventually broached the subject of time off.

'Of course, Emma,' he said smoothly. 'Your contract was for a five day week, flexible naturally, but we should be able to manage without you next weekend.'

'Thank you.' Emma felt her heart lift, and later in the day she telephoned Celia to tell her the news.

'Get your glad rags on,' Emma laughed. 'We'll do the town on Saturday.'

* * *

The week passed uneventfully. There was a steady stream of customers, some just curious, others willing to spend and sample. The figures began to look good on the computer, and Emma set up reports on each project so that at the end of the month they could evaluate income.

It was late afternoon on Friday that Alex approached her. 'When were you thinking of travelling, Emma?'

'I thought I'd catch the early train on Saturday.'

Blake had been listening and interrupted. 'Actually, Alex,' he said, his voice casual, 'I was thinking of going up to town myself for the weekend. It's quite a while since I stayed in London. I can give Emma a lift.'

'Do you think that's wise, Blake?' Alex's voice was cool and Blake coloured. Alex glanced at Emma as she made an indignant noise. 'I didn't mean giving you a lift, Emma. I was actually going to offer that myself. I have some business to attend to and I thought we could travel together.' He turned to Blake as Emma looked startled. 'I really feel you should stay here this weekend if you don't mind, Blake. With Emma and myself away, we need to leave someone in charge. Perhaps next weekend?'

The two friends were glaring at one another, and Emma was surprised by the sudden tension in the room.

'As long as you allow me to go sometime soon,' Blake muttered.

'Of course,' Alex said smoothly.

He was still staring at Blake, who soon dropped his eyes, shifting uneasily in his chair. There was something more behind the disagreement than a weekend off, Emma was certain, but her mind was still wrestling with the idea of travelling to London with Alex.

He turned back to Emma. 'Shall we say seven in the morning? I can drop you very near Kensington, which is, I believe, where you live, and then continue to my meeting.'

'That will be excellent, thank you.' Emma's voice was slightly breathless, and she hurriedly returned to the letter she was typing. 'I'll be ready.'

'Good.' Alex left the office, and Emma stared at the still-scowling Blake. 'I'm sorry, Blake. I didn't know you wanted this weekend off.'

He shrugged, and a wry smile cleared the frown lines. 'It doesn't matter. Another weekend will do just as well. I felt like a break, that's all, but Alex is the boss!'

He returned to his paperwork, and Emma was left wondering.

★   ★   ★

She hardly slept that night. After packing a small case she lay in bed, staring at the moon as it lit her window, and thinking of four whole hours spent with Alex in the confines of his car. And she had intended to go to London to clear him out of her head!

Eventually she dozed off, and was awoken by the alarm. Yawning, she showered and grabbed a cup of tea and piece of toast. She was in the hall five minutes early and waited with some trepidation for the appearance of Alex.

'Right, Emma.' He smiled at her blandly as he came down the stairs. 'Shall we go?'

Picking up her case, she followed him into the misty morning.

5

The car was luxurious, and as Emma settled in her seat she couldn't help a deep sigh of contentment. She loved travelling, and a journey in a BMW was not to be disregarded. As they passed Jumbo's field, she repressed a smile, but Alex's face was impassive as he slowly manoeuvred the narrow lane. The road was quiet at this time in the morning, and Leigh Manor and Kestleigh were soon left behind as they headed for Gloucester and the motorway.

Alex relaxed as the car moved smoothly into the overtaking lane. He turned with a brief smile at Emma. 'Well, what do you think of Herefordshire?' His voice was polite.

'Leigh Manor is very impressive,' Emma replied. 'I spent many summers when I was a child on my uncle's farm on the other side of the county, so I know the area a little.'

'Does he still farm?'

Emma shook her head. 'He sold it when he retired. He was my father's older brother and had no children, so the farm passed out of the family.'

'It's often the way these days,' Alex commented. 'Many of the farms round here are being sold, usually for financial reasons.'

'You're happy with the way Leigh Leisure is progressing?' Emma asked. She felt at ease in Alex's company in the cosy confines of the car.

He smiled. 'I think so. The potential for this type of development is enormous. Likewise, the loss would be enormous if it failed.'

'I can't see it doing that,' Emma murmured. She doubted that anything Alex put his mind to would fail.

'We'll see. It's early days yet.' He manoeuvred another overtake and they sped away through the traffic.

'Whereabouts in Kensington do you want me to drop you?'

'Are you sure it won't be out of your way?'

Alex shook his head. 'I've booked in at a hotel close by, and my meeting is in that area, so it's no bother.'

'Pontin Road, off the high street. There's a block of flats there.'

'I know it.' Alex glanced sideways at her. 'You live alone?'

'With my friend, Celia. My father and mother travel most of the time. He's a writer and always off to strange places. My mother follows with her painting paraphernalia.'

'And you haven't followed in their footsteps?'

Emma shook her head. 'I travelled with them when I was a child, obviously. I loved it, but unfortunately I haven't a streak of creativity in me.' She grinned ruefully. 'I take after my grandfather — he was very clever in the world of finance and I'm told I have his business brain. He's been a tremendous help to me over the years.'

They discussed Leigh Manor and its

future, and Emma felt excited by Alex's enthusiasm for his project. The fact that he was sharing his dreams with her spread a glow through her, and for the first time she felt she was part of that scenario. As details were revealed, she had a deeper insight into the long-term plans than she had acquired previously, and she stored up the knowledge as it was imparted. Alex was good company, and she couldn't help wishing the relaxed man who was chatting by her side would appear more often in the office.

'And you, Alex?' she ventured. 'Where were you brought up?'

He frowned for a moment and then glanced at her briefly. 'London,' he replied at last. 'My father was in finance, too. He's retired now, always wheeling and dealing. I spent quite a few of my early years around the stock exchange.'

'And now?'

'Now I'm enjoying the comparable peace of Leigh Manor.' He grinned.

'I've still some investments in London, but a few years ago I decided I needed a change, a new challenge and a breath of clean fresh air. Leigh Manor gives me all of those.'

Emma noticed he hadn't mentioned his mother, but decided she had pushed his confidences enough. With a sigh of contentment, she settled back and stretched her legs. The journey sped by, and she was almost sorry when they joined the slow queue of London traffic.

'We're here,' Alex commented at last and turned into Pontin Road, pulling up outside the flats. 'Shall I pick you up on Sunday, about four o'clock?'

'That would be wonderful, Alex, thank you.' Emma smiled as she opened the door. 'Flat number seven. If you press the intercom I'll let you in.'

'Fine.' Alex was looking into his mirror. 'See you then.'

She shut the door, and Alex pulled deftly into the stream of traffic without a backward glance. Entering her pass code, she let herself into the building and opened the door to her flat. There was a note from Celia; she had a pre-arranged interview but would be back for lunch. Leafing through her mail, Emma wandered around, trying to get her bearings. It felt strange, and she suddenly realised she was missing Leigh Manor. Smiling wryly, she made coffee and waited for Celia's return. The whole purpose of the visit had been to distance herself from Alex and Leigh Manor, but the journey to town had made that even more difficult than she had anticipated.

Celia was ecstatic to see her and talked non-stop as they hailed a taxi and headed for their favourite Italian restaurant for lunch. Over the red check tablecloth, Emma faced a barrage of questions from Celia.

'Well, what's Leigh Manor like? And Alex Baron? And the rest of the staff?'

'Hold on, Celia.' Emma laughed. 'Give me time.' She twirled her pasta on her fork and stared at it thoughtfully.

'Leigh Manor is beautiful,' she said at last. 'A lovely old manor house; and the new project, Leigh Leisure, is extremely exciting. It's going to be successful, I should say.'

'So tell me all about it.'

Emma filled in the details and Celia listened, interrupting now and then with a question. 'And what about Alex Baron?' Celia persisted as they sipped their coffee. 'What's he like?'

Emma hesitated. 'Well, he's a mixture. I thought him arrogant and impossibly rude at first.' She grinned as she remembered her encounter with Jumbo.

Celia giggled. 'Tell me again,' she insisted.

Emma did, with a great many embellishments. Time had lessened the fright of her adventure and she enjoyed recounting the humorous side, particularly Alex's reaction.

'He was so angry at first, I thought I'd be on the first train home.' Emma smiled. 'But after that, we seemed to get along well. When we discuss work we're really on the same wavelength. Then, of course, there was the fracas with Frank.'

'Your Frank?' Celia's eyes opened wide. 'What happened?'

Emma sighed and her voice sobered as she told Celia about the scene in the office. Celia watched her speculatively. 'And you think you can stay at Leigh Manor, now that Frank's involved?'

Emma nodded. 'I don't think Frank's going to visit often. Blake seems to conduct most of his business with him in London, so there shouldn't be a problem.' She wasn't sure who she was trying to convince, but she was determined not to run away from Frank again, at least not yet.

'Well, considering the reason you left London was because of Frank, there must be something pretty attractive about Leigh Manor to keep you there if he has his fingers in the place.' Celia was watching her shrewdly. 'It wouldn't have anything to do with Alex Baron, would it? He whose details have been very sketchy so far?'

Emma felt a blush rise in her cheeks and looked away. 'He's an attractive man,' she admitted, her voice casual. 'But he's already spoken for by the neighbouring farmer's daughter, Diane. I wouldn't like to cross her and poach her property. Anyway, it's not a good idea, and besides, he's not interested. Another coffee?'

'Hmm.' Celia was watching her friend. She knew her well enough not to pursue the subject, but she also guessed there was more to Emma's feelings than she was admitting.

'Hey,' Celia changed the subject, 'I've just had a tremendous idea!'

'What?'

'How about I do an article for *Country Pastimes*? It'd be ideal. I'll speak to my editor this afternoon. I'm sure he'll give the go-ahead. You can ask Alex and then I can come down for a couple of days. Then I can see for myself what's going on at Leigh Manor.'

'Oh Celia, would you?' Emma's eyes were shining. 'That would be terrific. I'll broach it to Alex on the way home and let you know. He's keen on publicity so I'm sure he'll be delighted. It's just what Leigh Manor needs.'

★　★　★

The weekend passed quickly, and all too soon it was Sunday afternoon. Celia had rushed off to do an interview, leaving Emma alone. Repacking her small case, she heard the doorbell ring. Surely that wasn't Alex already? If so, he was early.

Pressing the intercom, she heard Tony's voice. 'Can I come up?'

'Of course.' She pressed the release button and heard the front door open.

'Tony, this is a surprise.' She spoke quietly, aware of their awkward parting.

'Let me first say I'm sorry, Emma.' He smiled wryly. 'I was selfish. I realise how hurt you were, and I do understand, but losing you was a shock.'

'Forget it, Tony. It's lovely to see you.'

Emma gestured to a chair. 'How are you? Tell me all the news. How's the business?'

Tony held up his hand and laughed. 'Gosh, Emma, how I've missed you. The business is fine. You were right — it'll survive without you, but under protest. I've just completed another lucrative deal in Germany; I've taken on another client who wants to invest in this country. All exciting stuff. Are you sure you won't come back?'

Emma shook her head. 'Not just yet, Tony. I'm enjoying the challenge in Herefordshire. It's a brilliant scheme and would do your financial brain justice.'

'Oh?'

'Diversification of an old manor house, setting up working craftsmen and sales, a café, all the sort of thing that's popular at the moment. And there's still room for the prize cattle — and bulls,' she added, grinning.

'I have heard something about Leigh

Leisure,' Tony admitted.

'You have?' Emma was surprised and Tony nodded.

'You met Mike Talbot, I believe?' Emma nodded. 'Sang your praises all through our meal.' Tony was grinning. 'I must say I agreed with every word he said.'

Emma laughed. 'I remember him. Very interested and very knowledgeable.'

'He seemed rather impressed with the set-up, I must say. Rang me and asked me to meet him. Wanted to bounce a few ideas around.'

'Does he want to invest?'

Tony shrugged. 'Who can tell? We've worked together before. I like his style. Anyway, I'm seeing him again next week, so who knows what he may come up with.'

'Interesting.' Emma was looking thoughtful. It was strange how her old life was infiltrating her new, and the miles created no boundary at all.

At that moment the buzzer sounded

again and Emma let Alex in. 'I'm afraid I'm going to have to go, Tony,' she said regretfully. 'There's my employer now, come to collect me. Perhaps next time I come to town we can meet and have dinner?'

'I'd love to.' Tony stood up and buttoned his jacket. 'Don't leave it too long, Emma. I've missed your company.'

Emma answered the knock at the door and Alex walked in. 'Alex, meet Tony Merriman.' She turned to Tony. 'Alex — ' She stopped abruptly as Tony was grinning delightedly and rushed forward.

'Alex — Alex Baron! How marvellous. How are you, old chap?'

'You two know each other?' Emma was startled.

'We were at university together; studied at business college afterwards,' Tony explained. 'We were both going to make our fortunes.' He was beaming. 'We lost touch a few years ago. But it's great to see you, Alex.'

'You too, Tony. How are things? Pretty good, by the look of you.'

They were shaking hands and laughing as they exchanged news. Emma watched, bemused.

Tony's eyes were twinkling. 'So you're the predator that enticed away my best assistant.'

Alex grinned back. 'If I'd known she was your assistant, Tony, I'd have nurtured her company, not taken her away from your lucrative business. She'd have been more use as a spy.'

'Still the same unscrupulous Alex!'

'Hey, just a minute,' Emma interrupted indignantly. 'Don't forget I'm still here. I won't have you fighting over me.'

'We're not fighting, my darling.' Tony put an arm round her shoulder. 'I couldn't have wished you a better escape than with Alex. Could come in useful, though.'

'Escape?' Alex looked at Emma. 'Talking of which, we really must go, Tony. Here — ' He pulled a card from his wallet. ' — give me a ring at Leigh Manor. I might be able to put some business your way, if you have any suitable clients. We can have a chat, and next time I'm in town we'll arrange to meet.'

'I've already had my spies out.' Tony chuckled. 'Mike Talbot?'

'He's a colleague of yours?' Alex sounded amazed, and Tony nodded.

'He told me all about Leigh Leisure,' Tony said. 'But he failed to mention the owner was one Alex Baron.' He slapped Alex on the back. 'The news gets better and better.'

Tony followed them out as Emma locked up. Alex was quiet as he negotiated the London streets, and it wasn't until they were back on the motorway that he broached the subject of Tony. 'You worked for him, I gather?' His voice was thoughtful.

'For a number of years.'

'Why did you leave?'

'I needed a change,' Emma answered quietly. She couldn't bring herself to mention Frank again, and it didn't seem necessary.

The journey continued in companionable quiet. Emma broached Celia's idea. 'Celia works for the magazine *Country Pastimes*,' she said. 'She writes features for them, with photos of course, and she wondered whether you'd like her to do a double page spread.'

'Sounds interesting.'

'I thought it would be excellent publicity; the magazine's got a wide circulation. But I said I'd clear it with you first.'

'What does it involve?'

'She'd come and stay for a few days — in the village of course,' Emma added hurriedly. 'Do an interview, take photos.'

'Sounds simple enough,' replied Alex. 'I don't suppose it'll take up too much of my time. You can answer most of her questions.'

'Of course, if you want.' Emma was pleased at the prospect.

'And she can stay at Leigh Manor. We've plenty of guest rooms.'

'That's very generous of you, Alex. Celia will be delighted.'

'Anything for publicity.' Alex smiled. 'I'll leave you to arrange everything.'

Emma nodded and settled back in the comfort of her seat. Alex became lost in thought, and she enjoyed watching the countryside speed past. Arriving at Leigh Manor, she gathered her case and headed for her room.

'Janet's prepared a light meal in the dining room, Emma, if you're hungry,' Alex called after her.

Quickly unpacking and swilling her face, she decided a sandwich wouldn't go amiss. Descending the stairs, she approached the dining room. She could hear voices, Alex and Blake. They appeared to be rather heated, and she hesitated as she went to push the door open.

'Alex, that isn't fair.' Blake sounded angry. 'You can't use Emma like that.'

'I'm not using Emma, as you put it,

Blake.' Alex's voice was cool. 'I'm merely stating a fact. Emma worked for Tony Merriman. I know Tony well, and I know his business connections. All I'm saying is that Emma might prove to have some useful information that'll benefit Leigh Manor.'

'So you're prepared to 'soften her up', I believe was your expression, for the sake of information.'

'That wasn't what I meant, Blake.' Alex sounded exasperated.

Emma didn't wait to hear any more. She was fuming. So Alex was prepared to use her friendship with Tony to help his business deals, was he? She'd see about that! If he wanted to reinstate his friendship with Tony, that was fine but, 'soften her up'? She glared at herself in the mirror. 'I've a good mind not to ring Celia,' she muttered. 'Sod the publicity. Damn you, Alex Baron, damn you!'

Weary tears started and she brushed them away angrily. Now she would have to go to bed hungry!

6

Emma slept fitfully that night and felt weary as she switched on her computer the next morning. The conversation that she had overheard echoed around her head and she thought about resigning.

Resolutely, she concentrated on the morning post. Mid-morning Alex appeared. Emma gave him a brief smile and returned to the screen.

'Good morning, Emma.' He sounded cheerful and smiled pleasantly at her. 'Have you phoned your friend yet about the feature?' He leaned over her desk and Emma felt herself stiffen.

'No, not yet.' Her voice was cool, and her eyes when they met Alex's were sparking. 'I'll do it later.'

He looked taken aback at her tone and stood up. 'Of course. Whenever it's convenient.' His voice turned cold, and he cast her a puzzled look as he crossed the room to Blake.

Emma could feel anger coursing through her. Did he really think that she would compromise any of her previous acquaintances? He really knew nothing about women.

As she worked, she thought about Celia. Perhaps, after all, she would ring her and arrange for a visit. Celia had always been so sensible when it came to emotional problems. If she told Celia about the exchange between Alex and Blake, Celia would come up with some positive plan of action. She cheered up. Yes, that was what she would do. The sooner Celia arrived at Leigh Manor, the better, and Emma could enjoy a heart-to-heart.

As soon as she had finished lunch, she headed for her room. She rang Celia and was delighted that her friend could manage to come down at the end of the week.

'I'll get Blake to meet the train on Thursday,' Emma said. 'Just let me know the exact time. Oh Celia, it'll be wonderful to see you.'

'I only saw you yesterday,' Celia remarked, slightly worried by her friend's tone. 'Is everything all right?'

'Fine,' Emma said. She didn't want to discuss Alex over the phone. 'I'm just feeling rather lonely at the moment.'

'Chin up, old girl. I'll see you in a couple of days.'

Emma returned to the office in a more cheerful frame of mind and informed Blake of Celia's impending visit.

'Alex told me about the feature,' Blake said. 'It seems an excellent idea. I'll certainly meet Miss Dutton. I'm sure her visit will be fun.' His eyes twinkled. 'By the way,' he added, his voice casual, 'has Alex upset you?'

'Upset me?' Emma was taken aback and felt the colour suffuse her cheeks. 'Why do you ask?'

'Well, he seemed to think that you and he were getting on extremely well yesterday, and then suddenly this morning you were almost curt.'

Emma fiddled with some paperwork. 'I wasn't feeling too well this morning,' she mumbled without meeting Blake's eyes.

'Hmm.' Blake watched her shrewdly and then shrugged his shoulders and turned away. Emma heaved a sigh of relief and returned to the accounts.

She didn't see Alex again until she went down to dinner that evening. He was in the dining room, his back to her as she entered, staring out of the window.

'Ah, Emma . . . ' He turned as she closed the door. 'I hear Celia's arriving on Thursday?' Emma nodded. 'That's excellent.'

He was watching her closely, and she tried to keep her face expressionless.

'I thought we'd have a meeting at the end of the month, if you could get some figures on the various enterprises. Let's see which project looks profitable and which may need some sort of change.'

'That should be no problem,' Emma

said coolly. 'I've already set up reports and the bank statements come in every week, so we should have a good idea how we're progressing financially.'

Alex cocked his head to one side and his eyes bored into her. 'Have I said something to upset you?' he asked abruptly.

Emma shrugged and stared out of the window at the mellow evening.

'Out with it,' Alex said brusquely. 'I can't go on discussing work with you shooting arrows from those green eyes.' His voice was light, but there was underlying steel in his tone. 'You didn't come down last night. Was it something I said on the journey?' His tone was showing a hint of impatience. 'For heaven's sake, Emma — ' He sounded exasperated as she continued to stare through the glass. ' — if I've done something wrong, tell me!'

She turned to look at him as he ran his fingers through his long hair. His temper was beginning to mount.

'I did come downstairs,' Emma said

finally. 'You and Blake were discussing future strategy.'

'And?' Alex's face was blank.

'Apparently I'm worth 'softening up' because of my contacts,' Emma finished, her voice bleak. 'And I object,' she added, aware that she sounded like a petulant child.

Alex stared at her for a moment and then threw back his head and roared with laughter. 'Emma . . . ' he said at last, still grinning, as she stared at him stonily. 'Oh Emma, what *am* I going to do with you?'

She was nonplussed. This was not the reaction she had anticipated.

'I might have said you knew some useful people, I admit,' Alex said gently. 'I was amazed to find out you'd worked with Tony Merriman, and it was great to see him again. But 'soften you up'?' He chuckled. 'Believe you me, I know enough influential people myself without your help. I wouldn't dream of softening you up because of your friends.'

Emma was beginning to feel a fool.

She hadn't thought of Alex's many business connections. After all, he and Blake had managed to get Leigh Leisure up and running without her help. And he had known Tony previously. She was being too sensitive, she realised now, and that wasn't like her at all.

'So what did you mean?' Emma asked.

'I merely informed Blake of my meeting with Tony. I said a renewed friendship, possibly a business relationship, would be useful, and I intended to follow it up. I did express surprise at the financial world you'd worked in. I didn't realise your experience was of such a high calibre — very useful to us, I might have added.' He was smiling wryly at Emma, but his eyes still held annoyance. 'It was Blake who took my words the wrong way, and if you'd stayed and eavesdropped a while longer, you would've heard me put him right.'

Emma blushed and was lost for words. 'Oh,' she said lamely.

'Now can we stop all this nonsense and for goodness sake get on with the matter in hand? It's proving to be hard work having you as my assistant, Emma, it really is. And you're trying my patience to the limit.'

His eyes glared down into hers and she caught her breath. For a moment she felt herself drowning in his look and her heart skipped a beat. The tension flashed between them and she heard him suck in his breath.

'I'm sorry, Alex.' Her voice quivered and she dropped her eyes as the door opened and Blake walked in. He stopped for a moment and stared at them, the tension in the room tangible.

'You two at it again?' he said lightly. 'At the rate you're going on, it'll be pistols at dawn before we're finished. That should make for good publicity.' He pulled out a chair. 'Janet's on her way. Can we eat in peace, or hasn't the argument finished?'

'It's finished,' Alex said abruptly. 'Emma?'

He held out a chair and she sat down gratefully. She was surprised to find she was shaking, and as Janet entered with the tray she fiddled with her cutlery and sighed. At least the air had been cleared, but she was left feeling distinctly foolish, and that rankled.

* * *

She worked hard for the next couple of days, anxious to remain in Alex's good books, and disturbed by her arguments with him. She had never argued with an employer in her life the way she had with Alex, and she found it extremely disconcerting.

On Thursday she saw Blake leave to fetch Celia, and she had never felt so excited about seeing her friend. Janet had prepared a guest room in the same corridor as Emma, and she looked forward to spilling out her concerns in the evenings. She heard the Land Rover pull onto the gravel and left her desk. Opening the front door, she gave Celia a welcome hug.

'Celia, it's wonderful to see you. Shall

I take her up to her room, Blake?'

He smiled and sighed. 'I was hoping for that pleasure.' His eyes were twinkling. 'But you carry on, Emma. I expect you ladies have plenty to talk about.'

Emma led the way. 'I mustn't stay long, Celia. It is a working day, after all. I'll leave you to unpack and get settled in. There's only a couple of hours to go, and then I'll come and fetch you for dinner and we can have a gossip.'

'Fine.' Celia was looking around. 'This is extremely elegant, Emma, for an old manor house. I'm very impressed. I'll freshen up and go and see Alex. Blake said he'd be waiting for me in his study, so I'd better have a bit of a chat before dinner. I'll see you later.' She gave Emma another hug. 'My, but it's good to see you again, Emma. The flat seems awfully empty without you.'

Emma returned to the office, her heart light. Having Celia there would make a tremendous difference. Perhaps she might even get on with Alex for a few days.

Blake looked up as she entered. 'All settled in?'

'I've left Celia unpacking. I must finish these accounts so that I can do Alex's reports.'

'She's an attractive woman.' Blake was looking thoughtful. 'Have you been friends for long?'

Emma nodded. 'Since we met at college. We just clicked somehow, and when we left we decided to buy a flat together; get ourselves on the property ladder, you might say.'

'She's got a glamorous job, working with *Country Pastimes*.'

'Don't you believe it.' Emma laughed. 'Interviewing people isn't all fun. It can be very hard work, and she's to work some very unsociable hours. She's at the mercy of her interviewees.'

'All the same, it must be interesting.'

'Oh, it is, and Celia loves it.'

'Is there a man in the picture?'

Blake's voice was casual and Emma glanced at him. His face was the picture of innocent enquiry, and she smiled.

'Not at the moment. Work takes priority with her time.'

'Hmm.' Blake was concentrating on some paperwork. 'Interesting.'

The time flew by, and soon Emma was shutting down her computer. The reports were complete and she gave a satisfied sigh. 'Gosh, I'm starving.' She smiled at Blake and left to fetch Celia. She tapped on Celia's door and entered at her bidding.

'Well?' Emma plonked herself on the bed and watched as Celia smoothed her immaculate bob.

'Well,' Celia said, smiling at her in the mirror, 'two very attractive men. No wonder you want to stay here.'

Emma gave her an indignant look. 'The men have nothing to do with it. Blake is extremely nice, but not my sort at all — and Alex, well . . . ' She paused as her colour heightened. 'He's far too prickly for me.'

'Strange.' Celia was applying lipstick. 'Alex said the same about you.'

'He what?'

'He was asking about our friendship, and he happened to mention that he found you rather touchy to work with.' She smoothed her lips. 'I told him I couldn't understand it; that it was most unlike you.'

'Thanks,' Emma said drily.

'So what's with you and Alex?' Celia looked at her speculatively.

Hesitantly, Emma told her about the eavesdropped conversation. Even to her ears it sounded petty, and Celia stared at her with raised eyebrows.

'Must be the countryside getting to you,' Celia said quietly. 'Or the man?' she added with an enquiring look.

'What do you think of Blake?' Emma asked, changing the subject.

'Ah, Blake.' Celia's eyes twinkled. 'Very charming, very good-looking, but I'm not sure whether I'd trust him. But attractive, oh yes.' She grinned. 'Put it this way — I think I'm going to enjoy my stay. Pity it's only for a few days.'

'How long are you staying?'

'Tomorrow I shall interview the

residents of the barns and get a feel for the working environment. Saturday and Sunday I'll devote to Alex and Blake, although I'm hoping you and I might spend some time together. Johnnie comes down with his camera on Saturday for the day. It shouldn't take him long. I'll have all the angles set up, and he'll drive back that evening. I've checked the trains, and I'll catch the four-thirty on Sunday evening.'

'So let's make the most of the weekend,' Emma said. 'Lunch out Saturday?'

'All being well,' Celia agreed. 'If I can spend a couple of hours with Alex in the morning and then hand over to Johnnie, I can write up the copy in the afternoon. If there's time, we'll grab a lunch break.'

'Great.'

The friends made their way downstairs. Dinner was a pleasant occasion. Both men seemed interested in Celia's work, and Emma sat quietly in the background and watched as Blake hung on to her every word without any attempt to cover his admiration. Alex was less enthusiastic, but his eyes were speculative as they rested on Celia, and Emma felt a sudden pang of jealousy. If only he would show the same interest in her.

She smiled to herself as she realised her thoughts and concentrated on her meal, thankful that for once she could relax and there were no hidden undercurrents.

* * *

Celia disappeared among the buildings the next day, armed with tape recorder and a winning smile. Emma settled to check the financial reports she had compiled. Printing them out, she perused the figures. Each project looked to be holding its own; Tom, the potter, just ahead of the other workers in profit. She frowned as she noted the balance on Frank's painter, Josephine. The figure was very low.

Printing out the detail, she scanned the income. There was definitely something missing. There wasn't a single entry for rent or any other utility payment. She had understood from Blake that Frank was to pay a month in advance, but there was no sign of this amount.

She sighed. Surely she wasn't going to have trouble with Frank. She knew he was an unscrupulous person in some areas, and ruthless when it came to business, but surely he wouldn't withhold the rent at this stage in the project. Would he?

At that moment Blake entered.

'Blake . . . ' Emma hesitated, choosing her words carefully. 'Your agreement with Frank Lander. How was the rent to be handled?'

'Oh.' Blake sat in his chair, a frown on his brow. 'Didn't I tell you? He's paying a lump sum directly to Alex.'

'He is?' Emma looked mystified.

Blake nodded and shuffled some papers. 'Don't worry, Emma, there's no problem.' He smiled at her brightly and then bent his head to his work.

'But Blake . . . ' She hesitated again. 'The lump sums to Alex . . . '

'Yes?' He was tapping his pen on the table, his eyes on the screen in front of him.

'Are they being paid into one of the business accounts?'

'Of course!' Blake answered irritably.

'Which one?'

'How on earth should I know? For goodness sake, Emma, what is this? Don't you trust Alex?'

'It isn't that,' Emma answered quickly. 'I just need the figures so I can get a true picture of Frank's project.'

'May I suggest you do a report on the figures you have got?' Blake was staring at her coldly. 'I don't think Alex will take too kindly to your doubting his integrity.' His fingers moved over his keyboard and his attention returned to the screen.

Emma frowned as she surveyed the figures once more. If Blake said use the figures she'd got, then that was what she'd do. But if Frank were paying the rent directly to Alex, then that would distort the report. Did she dare question Alex? Frank Lander was a sore subject, and she was better avoiding mention of him if at all possible.

No. She sighed and put the report in the file with the rest. She'd best leave well alone. If that was the way Alex wanted it handled, then so be it. There was no way she could question his integrity on this subject. But she didn't like it, not one bit. She couldn't help feeling there was something dishonest going on, and that made her uncomfortable. Surely Alex wasn't creaming off some of the income? Her heart sank as she tried to assimilate the thought that Alex might be dishonest. Oh, surely not!

But the more her financial mind thought about it, the more she was convinced that Alex wasn't declaring all his income, and that meant fraud. She shivered and sighed dismally. What a dreadful end to a day that had started so promisingly.

7

Filing the papers away in her drawer, Emma turned to some correspondence.

'All right?' Blake eyes narrowed as he watched her frown.

'I suppose so,' Emma answered.

'Believe me, Emma, it's all above board.' Blake spoke quietly, but there was a finality to his tone, and Emma was surprised by the sudden look of anger that flashed across his face. 'Alex does business his way, and it's not a good idea to query what he does with his money.'

'Fine.' She was startled by the slightly threatening tone. 'I have no intention of questioning Alex. It's just that the figures aren't a true portrayal of the project, that's all.'

'I'm sure Alex will take that into account when he sees the overall report.'

Blake was smiling again now, and Emma stared at him. Sometimes she had the distinct impression that his charm and pleasantness were just a façade, and she wondered what he was really like under the skin. Occasionally he made her more uncomfortable than Alex, but there was nothing she could pinpoint; nothing that she couldn't put down to the sensitivity she seemed to have acquired since she arrived at Leigh Manor.

Emma smiled and returned to her paperwork, forestalling further conversation. But as she cleared the frown from her brow, she could feel Blake's eyes on her.

* * *

The evening meal was enjoyable. Celia was full of enthusiasm and plied Alex with questions.

'I'm very impressed,' she said as they sipped coffee. 'I've done quite a few features that have included diversifying, but this really is exciting. And it seems

113

to have got off the ground in record time.'

'That comes from Alex being a businessman at heart and not a farmer.' Blake grinned. 'He sees everything from a different level.'

'And you, Blake, what are you?' Celia's eyes were teasing as she turned to him.

'Well . . . ' Blake seemed to be pondering the matter. 'I think I was born a playboy.' They all laughed. 'Unfortunately, my parents didn't see fit to acquire a fortune before I was born, so some sort of employment is necessary to feed my expensive habits.'

'Expensive habits?' Celia asked and Emma saw Alex frown.

'Yes, well . . . ' Blake's voice cooled. 'I enjoy going to London as often as I can, but Alex here keeps me so busy that my visits are infrequent.'

Alex stared at Blake, who met his gaze defiantly, and Emma was aware of an undercurrent that passed between them.

'I'm sure I'm not as hard a taskmaster as Blake makes out,' Alex answered gently. 'But it's been a busy period.'

'Now that it's all going well though,' Blake said thoughtfully, 'perhaps I could take next weekend off?'

Emma was aware of the tension between the two men and frowned. The request seemed harmless enough.

'Of course, Blake,' Alex answered smoothly. 'You're entitled to a weekend off.'

Blake smiled triumphantly, and Celia, unaware of the undercurrents, clapped her hands. 'Oh Blake, that's great. Allow me to treat you to dinner on Saturday. Perhaps we could go on to a club?'

'That'd be fantastic.' He turned the full force of his charm towards her. 'I'm sure Celia will make sure I come to no harm while I'm away.'

His sarcasm was directed at Alex, and Emma watched the interplay. Alex showed no reaction to the comment, merely smiling and turning towards Emma.

'Perhaps in that case you ladies would enjoy Sunday dinner at The Jolly Duck? Shall I book a table?'

'What an excellent idea,' Blake agreed, and equilibrium was restored.

Later, in Emma's room, she and Celia discussed the men. 'I think Blake is rather lovely,' Celia said, blushing.

'Be careful, Celia. I'm not sure he's very trustworthy,' Emma warned.

'What makes you say that?'

Emma shrugged. 'He's very charming, I have to admit. But he was fawning all over Diane last time they were together. Not that she's interested in him. But I'm not sure he's the faithful sort.'

'Good grief, Emma.' Celia laughed. 'I'm only talking about the odd date or two. I hardly know the man, but a weekend in London with him as my escort would be fun. Other than that, well, we shall see.'

Emma smiled. 'Sorry, Celia. I don't mean to spoil your fun. Since I've been at Leigh Manor I've been decidedly edgy, not like me at all.'

'Anything to do with the gorgeous Alex?'

'The gorgeous Alex, as you call him, can be anything but gorgeous at times.' Emma sighed. 'He's not the type of man I want to get involved with.'

'Hmm.' Celia let the matter drop but she eyed her friend speculatively. She had a feeling Emma was already emotionally involved with Alex, whether she liked it or not.

*   *   *

Saturday dawned clear and bright, and Celia started preparing for her interviews and photographs. She would be spending the day working, so Emma decided to clear one or two outstanding items on her desk. There were also two new employees in the café to add to the payroll for the next week, so there was plenty to keep her busy.

There was no sign of Blake and she worked quietly through the morning. At last, fancying a coffee, she stretched and eased her aching fingers. As she stood, up the door opened. It was Alex.

'Still working?' He held a tray of coffee and Emma smiled.

'You must have read my mind,' she said lightly. 'I was just going to the kitchen in search of sustenance.'

'And here it is.' He lowered the tray onto a table.

As usual in Alex's presence, Emma felt herself tense. Mentally shaking herself, she turned away to stare out of the window at the sunshine.

'Coffee is served.'

Turning quickly, her foot caught on the edge of her chair, and before she could stop herself she tripped into the desk and then went sprawling across the floor. She felt a searing pain in her foot and lay there, winded.

'Emma.' Alex was beside her in an instant. 'Emma, are you all right?' He put his arm around her shoulders and tried to twist her into a sitting position. She winced. 'Where are you hurt?' His anxious voice was very close to her ear, and she was aware of the warmth of his arm across her shoulders. For no apparent reason she felt tears come into her eyes.

'My toe hurts,' she whispered forlornly, and then felt irritated as Alex suppressed a smile.

'Your toe?'

She nodded miserably, aware that she was making a fool of herself; and then she felt Alex's hand tenderly remove her shoe.

'You've split the nail,' he said, and she felt his fingers explore her foot. It was a delicious sensation and she forgot to be cross. 'There doesn't seem to be any other damage, but we'll get Janet to put a plaster and some ointment on it. It'll be sore for a couple of days. Now — ' He stood up and put his hands under her arms. ' — do you think you can stand up? And then you can sit in the chair and drink your coffee. That'll calm you.'

Carefully she let him help her to her

feet. Her heart was beating erratically, and it wasn't all with shock. Gently he lowered her onto the sofa that was reserved for guests against the one wall, and, sitting by her, he lifted her chin.

'All right?' His voice was gentle, and the concern in his eyes made her heart somersault. She nodded.

'I think so.' Her voice wobbled slightly. 'It's just my toe.' She managed a weak smile. 'It doesn't half hurt.'

Alex grinned and wiped a tear from her cheek. 'I think you'll survive.'

His eyes locked onto hers and she felt herself drowning in their dark depths. The tension between them was tangible, and for a second neither moved. Then, before Emma had time to drag her gaze away, his arm had tightened round her shoulders and she felt his ragged breath on her cheek. The next moment his lips were on hers, hot and demanding, and she let herself slip into the timeless ecstasy of his kiss.

How long it lasted she was never able to say, but the interruption was rude and sudden. 'Well, well.' Diane's voice was cold and grating. 'What a touching scene.'

Neither had heard the door open and Alex stood suddenly, leaving Emma confused.

'Emma fell and hurt her toe,' Alex said coldly. 'I didn't hear you knock, Diane.'

'Since when have I had to knock on your door, Alex?' Diane's voice was spiteful. 'And if Emma hurt her toe, may I suggest you were kissing better the wrong end of her body?'

Alex ignored her and turned to the bemused Emma. 'I'll go and ask Janet to fix a dressing.' His voice was cool, and Emma nodded dumbly.

Diane continued to stare at them both, her long pointed nails drumming on the desk.

'What do you want, Diane?' Alex asked testily.

'I was coming to see if you wanted to dine with me,' she replied, anger contorting her face. Emma shivered. 'But I can see you are otherwise engaged.'

Alex ignored the barb. 'I'm working, Diane. I'm not free today. However, Blake and I are taking Emma and Celia out to Sunday lunch tomorrow. You can join us if you want.'

'Who's Celia?' Diane looked startled.

'She's doing a feature on Leigh Manor for a magazine. She's been here for a couple of days.'

'I didn't know anything about that.' Diane's voice was steely.

'Why should you, Diane?' Alex's voice was equally cold. 'You can meet her tomorrow if you want.'

'And play gooseberry to your cosy foursome? No thank you.' She cast Emma a venomous look and flounced out of the room. The door slammed, and there was an uncomfortable silence.

'I'm sorry.' Emma sighed. 'I didn't mean to cause trouble between you and your fiancée.'

'Fiancée?' Alex rounded on her angrily. 'What on earth are you talking about?'

'Diane told me you and she were engaged,' Emma replied weakly.

Alex glared at her. 'We most certainly are not! I know Diane is keen to join our acres, but even *I* won't go as far as marrying someone to benefit Leigh Manor. In fact, I never want to get married. Women are nothing but trouble.'

He stormed out of the room, leaving Emma shaking her head in bewilderment. Women were trouble? Men seemed far more trouble, as far as she was concerned. Sighing, she allowed her mind to wander fleetingly to Alex's kiss. Did his last remark mean that it meant nothing? And he reckoned women were trouble!

Her reverie was interrupted by the arrival of Janet. 'Now then, ducky, let's have a look. Alex said you've hurt your toe.'

'It's not bad.' Emma grimaced as Janet's fingers explored her bruised foot. 'I was stupid, caught my foot and fell headlong. I don't know what Alex must think of me,' she said ruefully.

'He seems very concerned.' Janet was dabbing antiseptic on the injured nail and she cast a glance at Emma. 'In fact, he seems rather rattled.'

Emma grimaced. 'He's just had a row with Diane.'

'Oh, that one.' Janet dismissed Diane with a wave of her hand and unrolled some plaster. 'Take no notice of that madam. She's been trying to get her hands on Leigh Manor since she was old enough to think. And she doesn't care how she does it.'

Emma smiled. 'I don't think she's going to succeed somehow.'

Janet shook her head. 'Not with Alex, anyway. The person who traps Alex will have to be very special. After his mother, he thinks no woman is trustworthy, and that's a fact. Can't seem to get it out of his system, no way.'

'Perhaps if he falls in love he'll realise that all women aren't the same,' Emma murmured.

'If he allows himself to fall in love,' Janet replied tartly. 'There you are, love. That'll be a bit sore, but otherwise it should feel easier now.'

'Thanks, Janet, you're a gem.' Emma flexed her toe and gingerly worked her foot into her shoe. Limping slightly, she experimented across the office.

Left alone to her thoughts, she decided to call it a day. The rest could wait till Monday.

★　★　★

It was late on Saturday evening before the two friends had a chance to chat. Johnnie had completed his photo shoot and set off for London, and Celia was putting the finishing touches to her feature. Emma knocked on the door as Celia closed her laptop.

'I think that's all I can do before I get back to the office.' Celia smiled. 'I think it's going to be good, though. One of the most interesting features I've done, and we got some lovely shots today.'

'Of Alex?'

'Of Alex.' Celia laughed. 'When we eventually got him to smile.'

Emma thought ruefully of his morning and understood why Alex found little to smile about. But Celia could be very persuasive when she wanted to be.

'I shall look forward to seeing the completed feature,' Emma said.

'I'll send a copy for Alex's approval as soon as the proofs are ready. I expect you'll get a look at it then. I take it you're not coming home next weekend?'

Emma shook her head. 'No, I'll leave you in peace with Blake. But maybe the next one; I shall need a break by then.'

'Are you happy here?' Celia asked hesitantly.

Emma shrugged. 'Sort of,' she said quietly. 'I love the work and Leigh Manor, but sometimes the tensions are difficult.'

Celia was quiet for a few moments. 'So you're not returning to London just yet?'

'I don't think so. I've thought about it several times, but I think I'll stay for the summer at least, and then we'll see.'

Celia nodded, but she sensed an unease in Emma that worried her. The rotten business with Frank had taken its toll, and she wasn't sure that Leigh Manor was the calmest place to recover.

★ ★ ★

The next day the four of them piled into the Land Rover and set off for The Jolly Duck. Alex appeared in a cheerful frame of mind, and other than enquiring after her toe, he had maintained a silence about the encounter in the office. There was no sign of Diane, and for this Emma was grateful.

The restaurant was almost full and the clatter of happy diners filled the room. An appetising smell greeted their nostrils and they were escorted to a table in the large window overlooking the gardens.

'I'm going to enjoy this,' Celia said with relish. 'I shall miss all the attention when I go back.'

'What time is your train?' Blake asked.

'Four-thirty,' Celia replied. 'I'm all packed, so if you can run me to the station, Blake, I shall be grateful.'

'Of course,' Blake replied cheerfully.

'And thank you, Alex.' Celia turned her smile to him. 'Thank you for a most interesting few days. I've thoroughly enjoyed it. Your hospitality has been a bonus.'

'As long as the feature is extravagantly complimentary,' Alex said with a grin, 'it will all be worth it.'

'Oh it will be. You'll get to see it anyway before publication.'

They ordered their meal and Emma leaned back in her seat. She was trying to relax. Alex was deliberately avoiding eye contact and she couldn't help the spasm of disappointment that shot through her. It was as if yesterday's kiss had never happened. Ah well. She sighed and looked around.

The door of the restaurant opened again, and as Emma idly watched the couple coming in, she suddenly bit back a cry. Her whole body tensed, and she stared in absolute horror as she realised who the couple were.

The woman was staring around, and as her eyes rested on their table, Emma saw a gleam of malicious triumph shoot in her direction. Stupefied, she watched as they headed towards them. It was a startled Alex who realised her agitation first and swung round.

'Good grief!' His voice was incredulous. 'Diane, and Frank Lander.'

8

'Well, well, if it isn't Alex and party. What a surprise.' Diane's voice dripped venom. Frank was staring at Emma, who seemed unable to collect any coherent thoughts at all.

'Diane.' Alex had risen and his voice was coldly polite. 'And Frank. This is a surprise. Not business, I take it?'

'Not this time, Alex.' Frank's voice was equally chilly and his eyes swept the party sardonically. 'Although I might call on you later to review progress if it's convenient. Ah.' He turned as a waiter approached. 'Our table's ready, I believe. Come, my dear.' He took Diane's arm and guided her across the room.

There was total silence as Alex subsided into his seat. 'I didn't know Diane was on good terms with Frank.' He looked directly at Blake, who shrugged.

'Neither did I,' he replied quietly. His

eyes followed the couple anxiously.

Emma had been sitting, full of tension, her mind racing. What on earth was Frank doing here, and with Diane? Even Celia seemed nonplussed by the meeting.

'Does Frank visit often?' Celia was frowning thoughtfully as she looked at Emma.

'He came for the opening,' Alex answered. 'But I thought it had been arranged for all the business to be conducted in London.' Alex was glowering at Blake.

'It was.' Blake seemed as confused as everyone else. 'I knew nothing about this visit, believe me. Anyway . . . ' His voice had become irritated. 'I'm not the man's keeper, for goodness sake. He can do what he likes socially. Let's enjoy our meal and forget them.'

'Of course,' Alex said quietly as their food arrived.

But Emma found it very difficult to eat, the knot in her stomach making digestion impossible. She didn't glance in Frank's direction again, but she could feel his stare cutting through her like a knife and she felt afraid.

The happy mood was broken; and although Blake made an effort to rekindle the jollity, they were all glad when it was time to depart. None of them spared a glance for Diane and Frank as they left, and Emma heaved a sigh of relief as they headed back for Leigh Manor.

She bade a solemn farewell to Celia. 'Don't let that man get to you.' Celia was worried. 'Frank's a bastard. What his game is I don't know, but keep out of his way.'

'I intend to.' Emma smiled slightly. 'If I thought he was going to be around here for long, I'd come back with you. I just wish he'd let me go.'

'You ditched Frank. You're the first woman to do that, and Frank is not a forgiving man, we both know that. He's out for some sort of revenge, so just watch your back!'

Celia's words did little to restore

Emma's equilibrium, and she waved her friend off feeling miserable.

*   *   *

However, the week passed quietly with no sign of Frank or Diane, and Emma began to relax. Alex joined her several times in the office and arranged for a financial meeting the following Monday. Although aware of his close proximity, Emma discussed the business amicably with him, and without problems. In fact, she enjoyed their discussions, Alex's mind being keen when it came to business, and she felt the adrenalin quicken her thoughts.

Blake set off on Saturday morning, a smile on his face, and Emma cleared some paperwork before wondering what to do with her spare time. The sun shone, and she stood at the window watching the gardens sparkling and the early visitors wandering around. It was so peaceful here, and she couldn't help comparing the pace of life, though busy, with the frantic rush that seemed to dominate in the city.

'Penny for them?' She hadn't heard Alex enter and jumped.

'I was just thinking how beautiful and peaceful it is in the country,' she confessed.

'Not missing the city?'

Emma shook her head. 'Not at all.' She grinned. 'I miss my friends of course, but the way of life? Definitely not.'

'I was wondering if you feel like a walk.' Alex's voice was casual and she looked at him in surprise. 'I've got to go and inspect the cattle, and I want to check on one or two of the fences. It's such a lovely day, and you seem to have been cooped up in the office for most of your time.' He looked at her quizzically. 'The fresh air would do you good — and I might even introduce you to Jumbo.' His eyes were twinkling, and Emma laughed.

'How can I refuse an offer like that?' She tidied some papers and turned off the computer. 'Just give me a few minutes to change and I'll be with you.'

The walk turned out to be rather longer than Emma anticipated, but she enjoyed it thoroughly. The birds were singing in the hedgerows and the grass was springy beneath their steps. Primroses and cowslips scattered the fields and the sun was warm on their backs. The cattle grazed contentedly in a meadow on the riverbank, and Emma heaved a sigh of pleasure as they traipsed from field to field.

'I remember doing this with my uncle,' she said. 'We would walk for hours. Of course I was younger then and in better shape, but you forget the beauty of the countryside.' She smiled at Alex, who was striding along by her side.

'It's wonderful.' Alex took a deep breath and gazed into the distance. 'After working in the city for so many years, this place is an absolute godsend.'

'How long have you been here?'

'I bought Leigh Manor four years ago. Since then it's been hard work getting it back into shape. But at long last it looks as though we're getting there.'

'And will you stay?'

'I think so. I've come to love it here. I can't see any reason to move on at the moment.'

They continued in companionable silence, and Emma knew she would treasure this time together. She hadn't felt so happy and carefree in a long time, and it was a good feeling.

At last they returned to Leigh Manor and the bustle of the visitors. 'We seem to be attracting a good crowd,' Alex commented as they entered the building. 'Let's hope it continues through the summer. How about a coffee to finish the outing?'

'Wonderful.'

They sat in the kitchen as Janet bustled around the staff, who were baking cakes for the café, and Emma wallowed in the feeling of contentment that shrouded her.

On Sunday she phoned Celia for their usual chat. 'How was your date with Blake?' she asked.

'Well,' Celia began, sounding slightly worried, 'we had a wonderful afternoon together, and dinner was superb, but . . .'

'But?' Emma frowned.

Celia hesitated. 'Please don't say anything Emma, because I don't want to cause any problems, but we went to the casino afterwards. You know, Jake's, on the corner of the high street, where we all used to go when you were engaged to Frank.'

'I remember,' Emma said grimly. 'And?' she persisted.

'Well, Blake seemed to get rather carried away. I was a bit worried because he didn't seem to know when to stop. In fact, he lost an enormous amount of money.'

'Oh?' Emma was surprised. 'That doesn't sound like Blake somehow.'

'He made me promise not to tell Alex and laughed it off. I should say he'll have no problem settling the debt.'

Emma was remembering Alex's warnings to Blake when he said he was going to stay in London. Did Alex know Blake enjoyed gambling? Perhaps he'd been in trouble before. Emma shook her head. Blake was a grown man and not Alex's responsibility.

'So, other than that, did you enjoy yourself?'

'Oh yes.' Celia laughed. 'Blake's wonderful company. In fact, if I'm not careful, I could just agree to another weekend.'

Emma was pleased. It had been a while since Celia had shown any interest in a man, and Blake seemed ideal; except, perhaps, if he gambled. 'Maybe it was only once, and he got overexcited. You know how gambling can take hold. Has he been before?'

'He said not for a long while. He said it was just the excitement of the moment. He doesn't make a habit of gambling. How can he?' Celia laughed. 'I take it there are no gambling dens in Kestleigh?'

'Hardly!' Emma smiled. 'I'm glad you enjoyed it, Celia. Was there any sign of Frank?'

'No, thank goodness, none. Nor with you?'

'No. Where's Blake now?'

'He said he had some business to see to, and then we're meeting for lunch before he heads back.'

'Enjoy yourselves.' Emma put the phone down, smiling thoughtfully.

* * *

On Monday morning Blake was in the office before Emma and seemed in high spirits, blithely informing her that he'd had a great time with Celia.

'Fantastic lady, your friend,' he enthused as they waited for Alex.

Emma noticed he didn't quite meet her eyes as he talked, his hands moving restlessly through the paperwork on his desk. Although he seemed elated, she sensed a certain tension in his body. She smiled to herself. He was probably wondering if Celia had told her about his gambling, and probably regretting his hasty losses. But Emma had no intention of mentioning her conversation with Celia.

'Ah, Alex,' Blake said, relief in his voice. 'Here you are.'

Alex had his arms full of files and sat at the table between their two desks. He glanced casually at Blake as he sat down.

'Good weekend?' Alex asked. 'No problems?' He was watching Blake closely.

'None at all.' Blake rubbed his hands together. 'Celia and I had a great time.'

'Good.' Alex stared at him for a moment, and then, apparently satisfied, turned to Emma. 'Right, Emma, you have the reports ready?'

She nodded and handed him a sheaf of papers. There was silence for a moment as he scrutinised the figures.

'Hmm, the café seems to be well on target. The cakes sell well.'

Emma nodded. 'Janet's baking is very popular.'

'As far as I can see, Tom's doing well with his pottery, and James and Patti have a healthy turnover with their woodwork.' He frowned. 'Frank's artist isn't showing such promise.'

Emma said nothing. Was now the time to mention the outstanding monies, or the fact that Blake had said that Alex had a private arrangement with Frank? For some reason, she felt uneasy and waited in silence.

'Why are these figures so poor?' Alex was spreading Frank's report on the table. 'The paintings seem to be selling, yet the profits are low.'

Emma glanced at Blake, but he was staring out of the window, a frown on his face. She noticed his fingers were tapping uneasily on the desk; and with a sinking feeling in her stomach, the realisation hit her that Alex had no knowledge of the dues owed, otherwise he would have mentioned it by now. What on earth was she to do? Uncomfortably, she waited.

'Hmm.' Alex looked at Blake sharply. 'What's your arrangement with Frank regarding the rent and fees? He appears to be in arrears by rather a large amount.'

'He should have paid by cheque,' Blake answered, an innocent expression on his face, and Emma caught her breath. 'Is it not there?'

'No, it's not.' Alex was frowning and reached for the phone. 'We can't have this. If he's not honouring his commitment, we shall have to exclude him from the craft centre. We don't take passengers. Everyone else is managing their contributions, so he has no excuse to be behind. I should've known about this before.'

He shot an angry look at Emma and her heart sank. She glared at Blake, but he refused to meet her eyes.

'Frank, it's Alex. Sorry to bother you, old man.' Alex's voice was affable and he leaned back in his chair. 'Blake and I are going through the accounts, and somewhere along the line your rent seems to be missing. I understand if it's an oversight, of course, but I thought it better to remind you than have the arrears mount up ... What?' Alex frowned at Emma. 'You have?' His gaze swivelled to Blake. 'I'll sort it out.' His voice was grim. 'Leave it with me, Frank, and I apologise, I shouldn't have bothered you.'

He almost slammed the phone down and glared at Emma and Blake in turn. 'What's going on?' His voice was dangerously quiet. 'Frank said he sent the cheque to you a week ago, Blake?'

'That's right, he did.' Blake sprang up eagerly. 'I remember now. It came in with a pile of other cheques and I put it in your drawer, Emma, where I usually put them for banking.'

Emma stared at him in astonishment as he moved towards her desk, his eyes darting away from her face.

'Yes, I definitely remember now,' he

said, coming to Emma's side. 'It was in the drawer.'

He opened the drawer and stared in. It appeared empty, and Blake frowned.

'That's strange,' he said. Then he thrust his arm further into the drawer and triumphantly produced a long white envelope.

'Here it is.' He handed it to Alex.

'It's still here?' Alex opened the envelope, and there, sure enough, was a cheque in Frank's writing. 'Well, Emma?' Alex's anger was evident. 'Can you explain this? I've just made a complete idiot of myself with one of our investors, accusing him of not paying his rent, and here's the cheque — hidden in your drawer. Explain yourself.'

Emma stared at the cheque in horror. How on earth had she missed it? She checked her drawer carefully every day, and Blake had told her that Frank was paying the money separately, so she hadn't queried the fact that none was showing on the figures. Her heart turned to lead as she tried to grapple with the situation. What on earth was going on?

'I don't know,' she said weakly at last. 'I don't know how that got there.'

'It's obvious how it got there.' Alex's voice was heavy with sarcasm. 'What I want to know is why it wasn't banked. This is a great deal of money and would have put Frank's figures firmly in profit. Perhaps Frank was right and you're deliberately trying to sabotage his venture.'

'Sabotage his venture?' Emma's voice rose to a squeak. 'For heaven's sake, Alex.'

Alex shrugged. 'What am I supposed to think?' he demanded. 'One cheque only appears to have found its way to the back of your drawer, and it's Frank's. We all know how viciously you feel about Frank ending your engagement, but deliberately trying to oust his business from Leigh Manor is taking things too far. Way too far.'

Emma stared across at Blake. He was

shifting uncomfortably in his chair and she could see the high colour on his neck. Blake knew what was going on, that was certain. But how could she convince Alex of her innocence?

'Blake told me Frank was paying the rent and utilities directly to you,' she said in a low voice.

'Now why on earth would he do that?' Alex was running his hand through his hair in exasperation. 'What was I supposed to do with it, spend it?' He glared at Emma and she shrugged.

'I don't know,' she replied wearily. 'I just don't know.'

Alex rose. 'I don't think we can continue with the meeting at the moment. I might say something I regret.'

Glaring at Emma, he left the room. The door slammed.

'Blake?' Emma turned to him. 'Well?'

'Well what?' Blake attempted a smile.

'You told me not to worry about the rent when I queried it,' Emma said quietly.

'Did I?' Blake's face showed surprise.

'Perhaps that was because I'd already put the cheque in your drawer.'

'Had you?'

'Of course,' Blake said heartily. 'I'm sorry, Emma. It was an easy enough mistake. I shouldn't worry about it. Alex will calm down again. I'm going into Kestleigh later. I'll take the cheque to the bank myself.'

Blake still refused to meet her eyes and left the office without another word.

Emma leaned back in her chair and relived the events of the last hour. She shook her head. Doubts circled her mind, but she couldn't make head or tail of the situation. Just what *was* going on at Leigh Manor? And who could she trust?

9

Miserably, Emma got on with her work. She had a feeling this time Alex wasn't going to be lenient and she was likely to be dismissed. Her heart was heavy as she stayed in the office alone, still puzzling over the morning's events.

When the door opened she raised her head defiantly, ready for Alex's cold anger.

'Emma — what on earth's the matter?'

She felt tears threaten as she managed a weak smile. 'Tony, how wonderful to see you.' To his surprise, she flung herself into his arms and proceeded to drown his chest with sobs. He held her gently, his face a picture of alarm.

'Now then, what's all this about?' Tony's voice was gentle as, the storm of weeping over, Emma pulled away

sniffing and reached for her handker-
chief.

'I'm sorry, Tony.' Her voice wobbled.
'I don't know what came over me.'

'Obviously something is very wrong,'
he said sternly. 'This isn't like you at all.
Tell me who's upset you.'

She sank onto a chair and smiled
weakly. 'It's Alex and this job. I don't
think I'm cut out for it.'

'Nonsense. You're more than capable
of dealing with Leigh Manor, and Alex,
I should have thought. Good grief,
when you worked for me you tackled
far more complex issues than this.
What's Alex been saying?' He frowned
at her.

'I just seem to make so many
mistakes, and this morning . . . ' She
tailed off, blowing her nose.

'This morning?' Tony prompted.

Emma shook her head. 'It was
business, Tony. I can't tell you. I seem
to have made a terrible mistake, but
nothing makes sense.'

He raised an eyebrow.

'Anyway,' Emma continued, wiping her eyes, 'what on earth are you doing here, Tony?'

'I came to see Alex. I think I might have a client interested in investment here and I wanted to see the set-up for myself. He didn't tell you?'

Emma shook her head miserably. 'No. We had this row about Frank and then he walked out. I haven't seen him since.'

'Hmm, Frank.' Tony was looking at her speculatively. 'If Frank's involved then that explains a lot. Not a nice man, our Frank, especially when scorned.'

Emma smiled wanly. 'I'd noticed.'

'I don't know why Alex got involved with the man. Anyway,' he said, standing up, 'are you all right now? I think I'd better go and find Alex. I'll see you again later. Chin up, Emma; you'll win through.'

She doubted that very much; but as Tony left the room, she repaired her makeup and resolutely set about clearing the morning's post.

In Alex's study, Tony was repeating his question. 'What on earth possessed you to involve a man like Frank in Leigh Leisure?'

They were sitting across the desk from one another having discussed formalities, drinking coffee before they made an inspection of the premises.

Alex looked thoughtful. 'It was Blake, actually. I didn't know the man. Blake produced him and his artist as our first resident worker. Blake seemed to think he was ideal.'

'And you didn't check him out?'

Alex shrugged. 'If I can't trust Blake's judgment as my manager, then I shouldn't be employing him.'

'Then perhaps you shouldn't.'

'So tell me why not?'

'Frank's unscrupulous. I wouldn't say he was exactly dishonest, but he comes very close. And he has the most unpleasant personality.'

'Hmm.' Alex made no comment.

'I take it you know he was engaged to Emma?'

Alex nodded. 'And Emma walked out on him.'

Tony smiled grimly. 'Oh yes, but she had good reason. All her friends warned her about the man, but she thought she was in love. He's a control freak, he was also repeatedly unfaithful, and when Emma realised the truth, it broke her heart.'

Alex was frowning.

'She finally plucked up courage to finish with him, but he won't let go. No one, but no one, leaves Frank. He's the one that does the leaving; his pride won't allow otherwise. I don't know what sort of tale he's spun you, but Frank's the villain here.'

'I see.' Alex's face was thoughtful.

'And I think you'll find Frank has some hold over Blake, otherwise he wouldn't be involved in Leigh Manor. True, he was looking for a gallery for Josephine. Her work needs recognition. It's good, but the main galleries won't take a chance on her yet. But I think you'll find there's more to Blake's relationship with Frank than mere friendship.'

'Now you're telling me something I don't know. I'll look into it. This morning — '

'Yes, Alex, what did happen this morning? I popped in to say hello to Emma and she flung herself into my arms, sobbing her heart out.'

'She didn't tell you?'

Tony shook his head. 'Emma's too loyal for that. But it must've been something pretty drastic for her to react like that. When I employed her she was the epitome of self-control and reliance, the best secretary I've ever had.'

'Really?' Alex looked sceptical.

'The trouble with you, Alex old boy, is your attitude to women. You distrust them first and wait for them to prove you right.'

'Yes, well . . . ' Alex looked uncomfortable.

'Don't you think it's about time you

allowed yourself to forgive your mother?' Tony's voice was gentle. 'Maybe then you could form some sort of relationship with a woman. Emma's the most loyal, most trustworthy person I know; and I must say it grieves me to see her so unhappy.'

Alex was staring into his coffee.

'Have you ever thought of contacting your mother?' Tony asked suddenly. 'Maybe, if she could tell you why she left, you could put your anger aside?'

Alex shook his head. 'Why would she want to speak to me now, after all these years?' His voice was bitter.

'Why shouldn't she?' Tony answered mildly. 'What was your father's explanation?'

'He never spoke about her. I was told she'd left, and I was never to mention the matter again.'

'And you haven't? Ever?'

Alex sighed. 'My father didn't like disobedience. His temper was pretty frightening, especially to a young boy. I suppose I'm still a bit afraid of him, even now.' He smiled ruefully. 'I rarely see him; and when I do, we're never comfortable together.'

'Has it not occurred to you that your mother found his temper pretty frightening too?' Tony persisted. 'Don't forget, in those days we weren't as enlightened about domestic violence as we are now. Maybe your mother had no choice?'

Alex shrugged. 'She's had plenty of time to find me.'

'Maybe she's afraid to. I'll tell you what, Alex.' Tony leaned forward. 'Shall I make a few enquiries, see if she can be traced; and if so, we'll take it from there?'

Alex looked at his friend doubtfully. 'Is that a good idea?'

'I think it's an excellent idea, especially if it's going to make you more tolerant of women, and stop Emma howling all over my best suits.'

'Please yourself,' Alex growled, and Tony smiled to himself. At least Alex hadn't said no; and if he found his mother, well, he'd sort that problem out when he came to it.

'If you're sure.' Alex stood up. 'Now, that's enough of the lecture, Tony.' He grinned. 'Maybe I've misjudged Emma. I must admit she's been getting under my skin lately, but she is good at her job.' He sighed. 'And I'll explore the Blake and Frank scenario a bit further. Maybe I've been too lax in giving Blake his head.'

'Hopefully not.'

Alex took a deep breath. 'Let's go and have a look at Leigh Leisure in action. And Tony, I'd appreciate it if you wouldn't repeat this conversation to Emma.'

'Of course not.' Tony put his hand on Alex's shoulder. 'It's your mess to sort out, pal. I just don't like to see my best secretary and one of my best friends at loggerheads, that's all.'

'We'll sort it out. Thanks, Tony.'

* * *

In her office, Emma was still mulling over the catastrophe of the morning and thinking that her time at Leigh Manor would soon be over. She would ring Celia that night and arrange to go back to London for a long weekend. Maybe there things would look brighter. Bleakly, she stared out of the window.

It was mid-afternoon before she saw Tony again. Blake hadn't put in an appearance at all, and she felt incredibly weary. It was a relief to see Tony's cheerful face as he entered the office.

'Right, my girl, go and pack a case. You're coming home with me.'

'I've been sacked?' Emma gasped, her heart sinking.

Tony laughed and shook his head. 'Indeed not,' he replied. 'I've had a talk with Alex and persuaded him you need a few days' holiday. You and Celia can paint the town, or whatever you care to paint, and put Leigh Manor out of your head for a few days.'

'Really?' Emma stared at him incredulously. 'Are you sure?'

'Absolutely.' Tony was rubbing his hands together gleefully. 'Alex will be along to tell you himself in a minute. In the meantime, go and pack a case. You've got the rest of the week off.'

Emma needed no further bidding. Eyeing her desk doubtfully, she shrugged and then went to her room. Throwing a few clothes in her case, she was in the hall in a matter of minutes. Alex was talking to Tony. She approached them with some trepidation.

'Ah, Emma.' Alex smiled at her, his eyes twinkling. 'Tony's convinced me you need a break from my tyrannical bossing. I'm sure we can manage for a few days, so go and enjoy yourself.'

She gazed at him suspiciously. 'You're sure?'

He nodded. 'I've one or two things to sort out with Blake — and Frank. By the time you return next Monday, I should've cleared the air a bit. Perhaps then we can get down to some serious work without further conflict.'

Emma was about to protest and then

bit her lip. She desperately needed a break, and she wasn't going to jeopardise that chance by trying to defend herself. Let Alex sort it out.

'In that case,' she said, smiling gratefully, 'I'm ready when you are, Tony.'

★ ★ ★

The drive back to London was quiet. Tony seemed lost in thought, and Emma was glad to relax and lean her head back against the comfortable headrest as they sped along the motorway.

'What on earth did you say to Alex?' she asked once.

Tony grinned. 'I told him you were the best secretary that had ever stepped out of London.' Emma laughed. 'And that it was about time he stopped hating women,' he added.

'You've known Alex a long time?'

'We go back a long way. He's been a good friend, and I'd like to see him in a happy relationship. It's about time he let go of the past and looked around him. There's a perfect companion right under his nose, if only he could see it.'

Emma blushed. 'Well, thanks for the ego boost, Tony.' She smiled. 'But I don't think Alex is ever going to see me as relationship material.' Her voice was wistful, but Tony didn't comment further.

After he'd dropped her off, Emma let herself into the flat. Unpacking quickly, she stood for a long time in the shower, letting the warm water ease her aches. By the time she had dressed and made coffee, Celia's key sounded in the lock.

'Emma.' Celia crushed her in a bear-like hug. 'Tony said he'd try and bring you home.'

'He did?' Emma was startled. 'When?'

'I'll tell you all about it,' Celia replied. 'Let me just shower and change. Make coffee, there's a love, and I'll fill you in on what's been going on.'

Emma was mystified. It seemed that Celia and Tony had been hatching her escape behind her back.

* * *

Relaxing on the sofa, she poured Celia a mug of coffee and they both settled down.

'Well?' Emma leaned forward. 'What did you mean, Celia?'

'Tony called me the other day,' Celia began. 'He'd been at some conference and Frank had been there, bragging about his new venture at Leigh Manor. He also told Tony that you and he were getting back together.'

'He what?' Emma exploded.

'Precisely,' Celia replied. 'Anyway, Tony thought it highly unlikely and phoned me. I said of course not, and we both agreed we were unhappy with Frank being involved in Leigh Leisure. The reason you were in Herefordshire in the first place was to get away from him. Anyway, Tony spoke to some of his contacts and did a bit of fishing. I'm not sure what he discovered — I haven't heard from him for a couple of days — but he came to the conclusion that Leigh Manor wasn't the best place for you to be.'

'And then he arrived and found me in tears,' Emma commented thoughtfully.

'He did?' It was Celia's turn to be startled.

Emma nodded. 'I practically soaked his jacket,' she admitted sheepishly, and proceeded to tell Celia the saga of the missing cheque.

Celia frowned. 'It sounds to me as if you were set up,' she said at last. 'By Frank and Diane.'

'We did see them out together,' Emma said. 'But why?'

'Diane wants you away from Leigh Manor — you represent a threat to her plans for Alex and herself. And, of course, Frank wants you back in London so that he can pursue you again.'

Emma shuddered. 'There's no chance of my going out with him again,' she said grimly. 'I never want to set eyes on the man again.'

'You can't convince Frank, though.

His ego won't allow him to accept that.'

'He'll have to.' Emma's voice was flat.

'Anyway, let's not waste precious time on thoughts of Frank. I vote we go out for a meal, have an early night, and then perhaps tomorrow Tony will tell us what he's found out.'

Emma agreed to Celia's plan with alacrity; and that night, as her head touched the pillow, she slept dreamlessly for the first time in a long while.

* * *

Waking refreshed next morning, Emma reflected that Leigh Manor and its problems seemed far away, and she wondered if she'd go back. Celia had to work, so Emma pottered around the flat; and when the doorbell chimed towards lunchtime, she was pleased to hear Tony's voice on the intercom.

'Tony, come up.' She released the catch and he arrived, holding her at arm's length and studying her face.

'Well, I must say you look better than you did last night,' he said, grinning cheerfully. 'Was I right to rescue you?'

Emma laughed. 'Indeed you were, my knight in shining armour. I must admit I feel better, but I still don't understand what's happening at Leigh Manor. Did you really come to see Alex on business?'

'Most certainly.' Tony followed her into the kitchen as she filled the coffee percolator. 'I've a young artist, Dan — the next Picasso he's been called by some. Daubs oils in unintelligible splodges, and apparently his pictures are brilliant. I can't see it myself, I'm afraid — give me a good old country scene any time — but no one's prepared to take a risk yet on showing his work. He and his paintings are colourful, and I thought he could make a welcome addition to Alex's menagerie.'

'And was Alex interested?'

'He's thinking about it. He's already got one painter, thanks to Frank; but should Frank pull out, I definitely think he'll take young Dan on.'

'And is Frank likely to pull out?'

'Let's just say I'm working on it,' Tony said cheerfully. 'By the way, I'm also working on your friend, Celia. Delightful woman.'

'Tony . . . ' Emma laughed. 'I don't want to see Celia hurt.'

'Celia can take care of herself, and I have no intention of hurting her.'

'You'll have to work on getting Blake out of the picture, then.' Emma was smiling. 'There seems to be an awful lot of manipulating going on at the moment.'

Tony sighed. 'I think maybe Blake's days are numbered, unless Celia is completely in love with him. I think he'd be the one to give her grief if she continued with that relationship.'

'Why?' Emma asked sharply.

'Well . . . ' Tony hesitated. 'I suppose you'll find out sooner or later — I haven't told Celia yet, mind — but Blake is in a heap of trouble.'

'What sort of trouble?' Emma was alarmed.

'Financial.'

She stared across the table at him. 'Tell me,' she demanded.

'Gambling,' Tony stated baldly. 'Blake's always been a gambler. Never knows when to stop.'

'Celia said something along the same lines when he took her out last weekend. But I don't think she realises it's a serious problem.'

'I don't suppose she does. I have it on good authority that he has some heavy debts — and some of them are to Frank.'

'Frank?'

'And from what I've gleaned, Frank is out to make good use of Blake's indebtedness. Blackmail springs to mind.'

'Blackmail?' Emma looked at him in horror. Frank was blackmailing Blake? So where did Leigh Manor come in? And what about Alex?

10

Tony was fiddling with his spoon as Emma assimilated his words. 'How does Alex fit into all this?' she asked at last. 'And what are you going to do about Frank?'

'I need some proof before I can go to Alex. Alex is very loyal, and Blake's been his friend for a long time.'

'I think Alex might know about Blake's gambling,' Emma said slowly. 'Something he said when Blake was going to London ... I got the impression he was warning Blake about his behaviour.'

'Oh, I'm sure he knows about Blake's gambling,' Tony agreed. 'But I don't think he realises Blake is indebted to Frank. I must admit it's unlike Frank to do business so far from London; and unless he's getting something for free, then nothing would induce him to invest in Leigh Leisure.'

'So Blake is repaying him in some way, through Leigh Manor?'

'It looks like it. I've a few more favours to call in, so the set-up may become clearer. I intend to sort things out before you return to Leigh Manor. In the meantime,' Tony added, grinning suddenly, 'would you two ladies like to be taken out to dinner tonight?'

'Tony, that would be wonderful!' Emma smiled.

She followed him to the door. 'And Tony,' she said, catching his arm, 'thank you so much for all you're doing. It's wonderful to know I've got a true friend.'

'Don't worry.' He kissed her lightly on the cheek. 'You're very special, Emma, and I won't have a rat like Frank harming you. Besides, Alex is an old friend, and I think he's being bamboozled as well.'

'Even so, you're a gem.'

Tony's eyes were twinkling. 'Well there is, of course, the added attraction of the delicious Celia.'

Emma laughed and locked the door. She felt so much better already, and suddenly everything took on a different perspective. If Blake was in the power of Frank, then that could explain quite a lot; that, with the added vindictiveness of Diane, would put a whole new light on the picture. She wondered what Alex would make of Tony's accusations, and her eyes were worried as she thought of Blake. He seemed such a pleasant man. Perhaps he was; maybe his weakness for gambling had taken over his life.

Emma sighed. She would leave Tony to explain to Celia the morning's conversation, and then it would be up to her. Maybe she would decide to rescue Blake.

* * *

Celia was delighted with the dinner invitation, and the two women dressed in high spirits. With one of them on each arm, Tony swept into the restaurant.

'I'm certainly a lucky fella tonight.' He beamed at the waiter. 'Two gorgeous women to keep me amused. Now,' he said as he scanned the menu, 'what do we fancy?'

The meal was delightful, and Emma noticed how Celia's eyes sparkled when she talked to Tony. Perhaps there was a bond forming between the two. She smiled at the prospect. She had always been very fond of Tony, and she would be delighted if a relationship sprang up between him and her best friend. She suddenly thought of Alex, and wished he was there with them. The evening would then be perfect.

'Penny for them?' Tony had caught her wistful expression.

'Hardly worth that.' Emma coloured. 'I was thinking about Alex actually.' She felt the heat rise in her cheeks and stirred her coffee.

'Talking of whom . . . ' Tony leaned back, looking at Celia thoughtfully. 'I take it Emma hasn't filled you in on our conversation of this morning?'

Celia shook her head and turned to Emma. 'What conversation?'

'I thought it'd be better coming from Tony,' Emma said. 'He's the one who's been doing all the probing.'

Celia listened quietly as Tony explained about Blake's gambling and his involvement with Frank.

Celia sighed. 'I was worried last weekend,' she admitted. 'We went to the casino and he got rather ratty when I suggested he'd lost enough. I went to get a drink, and when I came back he had left the table; but he was very pale, though he laughed his bad luck off.'

'Apparently it's not the first time,' Tony commented. 'His gambling debts go back several years.'

'And Frank bailed him out,' Emma said bitterly.

'Frank would,' Celia put in. 'He likes to have a hold over people.' She looked meaningfully at Emma. 'And I suppose Leigh Manor is somehow involved?'

'We're not sure how yet,' Tony said. 'But I intend to find out.'

'Poor Blake,' Emma said softly. 'He obviously needs help.'

Tony escorted them back to their flat and promised to keep in touch.

*   *   *

The next day Emma went shopping. It was wonderful to have some time to herself, and Celia had promised to take the following day off so that they could have a day out together. Emma was tempted several times to ring Alex, but managed to restrain herself and purposefully put Leigh Manor and its problems out of her head. When she returned, there was a message from Tony on the answer phone.

'I've come up trumps,' the mysterious message said. 'I'm on my way to see Alex.'

The machine went dead and Emma stared at it, perplexed. How infuriating! Just what had Tony discovered? And how like him to leave a cryptic message that would leave them guessing.

Celia listened to Tony's voice when she returned that evening.

'How annoying,' she said, intrigued. 'What on earth does he mean?'

'I wish I knew.' Emma grinned. 'He's done that on purpose, to keep us in suspense. Aggravating man!'

They laughed and settled down for a quiet night in. Celia cooked omelettes and Emma opened a bottle of wine. They tried Tony's number a couple of times, and his mobile, but all they could do was leave messages. None were returned and eventually they went to bed, still puzzled.

It was late morning as they lazed over coffee, discussing in a desultory fashion what they were going to do with the rest of the day, that the intercom buzzed.

'Can we come up?' It was Tony's voice, and Emma smiled.

'I'm not sure you can, after that annoying message yesterday,' she replied, laughing. 'And who's 'we'?' she added, suddenly cautious.

'Me and a friend.' Tony would offer

no further explanation, so eventually Emma let them in.

Standing in the doorway with Tony was Alex. Emma was astounded. 'Alex, what on earth are you doing here?' He looked distinctly uncomfortable and avoided her gaze.

'He's come to eat humble pie.' Tony was grinning.

'Alex?' Emma was watching him closely, her heart thumping.

'Any chance of a coffee?' Tony asked. 'It's a long journey and we're gasping. Then all will be revealed.'

'Of course.' Celia hurried to the kitchen and Tony followed.

Alex gazed at Emma, his dark eyes unfathomable, but she was glad to see there was no anger there.

'I'm sorry, Emma,' Alex said simply. 'I've misjudged you.'

'You have?' Emma was taken by surprise.

'It seems so.' Alex moved towards her and took her hand in his. 'Can you forgive me for being such a brute?' He

174

smiled, and Emma felt her heart begin to race.

'Of course, Alex.' Her voice was husky.

At that moment Celia and Tony reappeared with a tray of coffee and biscuits. 'You've made your peace then?' Tony grinned at Alex as Emma snatched her hand away and they all sat down.

'Now . . . ' Tony handed round the cups. 'Shall I begin, or you?' He looked at Alex.

Alex sighed. 'It would appear I've been conned,' he said ruefully. 'Difficult for me to admit, but there it is.'

'Blake?' Emma asked, and Alex nodded.

'Blake and I go back a long way.' Alex sipped his coffee. 'We were at university together and we've always been firm friends. I knew he enjoyed gambling, but I didn't realise how addicted he'd become until I met him in London one day, about four years ago. I hadn't seen him for a while and he looked ghastly.

Eventually I discovered he was heavily in debt; so heavily, in fact, that he'd put the family home on the market.'

'The family home?' Celia said.

Alex nodded. 'Leigh Manor.'

'Leigh Manor?' Emma was astonished.

'Leigh Manor was Blake's family home,' Alex repeated. 'There was no other family to bail him out. I knew Diane and her father wanted to buy, and at the time there seemed a possibility that Blake and Diane would marry and so solve the problem.'

Emma listened as the pieces began to fall into place.

'Blake eventually realised that all Diane wanted was his land and that she didn't give a fig about him. I'd visited Leigh Manor in the past — I loved the place — and, although financially it was an encumbrance at that time, I could see the potential for diversification, and I thought, why not? It would be an interesting investment, it would help Blake, and it would thwart Diane in her plans for control of a ridiculous acreage. Blake agreed to remain as my manager. After all, he knew the place better than anyone. And there you have it.'

'See?' Tony was grinning. 'I said I'd uncover the whole story.'

'But how did Blake react to working for you as the owner of Leigh Manor?' Emma asked thoughtfully.

'He found it difficult,' Alex admitted. 'But he knew it was the only chance he had of remaining there in any capacity.'

'Janet knew?' Emma asked.

Alex nodded. 'She said nothing because she didn't want to see Blake reminded of the fact. She'd nursed him since a baby and couldn't bear to see him hurt.'

'And where does Frank fit in?'

Tony continued with the story as Alex stared into his cup. 'Apparently, unbeknown to Alex, Blake was running up more debts — and that's where Frank stepped in. Once he had Blake under his control, he could manipulate him at will. He'd heard about the new venture at Leigh Manor and wanted a slice of the action. He made Blake get him an introduction, came up with Josephine, and there you have it.'

'Not quite all,' Alex interrupted. 'The deal was that Frank shouldn't pay rent or utility expenses. I knew nothing of this arrangement, of course, and so all he would reap was profits. Quite a nice little scam.'

'And the missing cheque?' Emma was agog.

Alex smiled. 'That's where you come in. You'd already spotted the rent wasn't being paid. Blake admitted you'd queried it with him, and you were nosing around too much, so he wanted you out. Frank wanted you back, and at the same time you were thwarting Diane's plan B to take over Leigh Manor via myself. Then, the last time Blake was in London, he lost money again.' Alex looked at Celia and she nodded. 'So once again he went to Frank, who came up with the cheque fiasco. You would get the sack, Blake would rescue the cheque before it got banked and destroy it, and in the ensuing chaos the matter of Frank's debt to Leigh Manor could be forgotten. Only, it didn't quite work like that.'

Alex leaned back, and Emma sat digesting the implications of his words. 'And Blake?' she asked at last.

Alex sighed. 'Blake admitted everything,' he said sadly. 'He's now going to have to raise a loan to pay back his debts. I think Frank will probably be lenient in the circumstances and agree a settlement figure. But at least Blake's accepted he's addicted to gambling and something must be done. He's going to get professional help.'

'And his job at Leigh Manor?' Emma felt desperately sorry for Blake and the mess he was in.

'I've said that if he seeks proper help and can keep away from the casinos, I'll give him another chance. I shall keep my eye on things a bit more carefully. But I can't turn my back on him.' Alex poured more coffee. 'Gambling's an addictive illness, after all. The man can't help himself; he's sick. I'll help all I can, but I'm afraid it'll be a long time before I can trust him again.'

'Anyway,' Tony chuckled, 'Frank has been asked to remove Josephine; and I shall install Dan, my budding Picasso, as from next week. I'm sorry for Josephine, as none of this is her fault; but if she's talented, I'm sure she'll find somewhere else to display her work. I'll ask around and see if I can use my influence a little.'

'Good,' Emma said.

'And I'm hoping, Emma,' Alex said as he leaned towards her, 'that you'll return as well. I can't manage without you.'

She smiled and appeared to be considering his proposal. 'I might,' she said at last, a twinkle in her eye.

'What do you want me to do, beg?' Alex frowned and Emma laughed.

'Maybe,' she giggled.

He looked at her and Emma felt her

heart melt. She could hardly believe this was all happening — and the way Alex was looking at her . . . The message in his eyes couldn't be plainer.

Tony rose and nudged Celia. 'I'll help you wash up,' he said pointedly.

'Of course.' Celia hastily got to her feet and carried the tray into the kitchen. The door closed loudly.

Emma sat with her fingers twisting in her lap. 'That was rather an obvious ploy to leave us together,' she said breathlessly.

Alex stood and walked towards her, catching both her hands in his and pulling her to her feet. 'It was,' he agreed, his arms circling behind her back and pulling her close.

She felt the warmth of his body as it pressed against her, and just for a moment she resisted, but her emotion overcame her and she yielded as he bent his head and kissed her, his lips hot and demanding against hers. The flat slipped into oblivion and she forgot the other two in the kitchen. She forgot

Leigh Manor and all its problems. At last she was in the arms of the man she had loved from the moment he had rescued her from Jumbo; although it was only now, in this precious moment, that she could admit that.

The kitchen door banged again, and they pulled apart to the delighted chuckle of Tony.

'All's well that ends well,' he said. 'About time, too.'

*   *   *

The next morning, Alex and Emma returned to Leigh Manor in high spirits. The warmth in the car echoed the warmth in Emma's heart, and she leaned forward excitedly as they sped through Kestleigh.

'I feel as if I'm coming home,' she said.

'You are,' Alex answered, and touched her hand briefly. 'You are, Emma.'

Janet was waiting with a beaming smile and ushered them in to steaming coffee and chocolate biscuits.

'How long is this spoiling going to last?' Emma chuckled.

'For all of ten minutes.' Alex grinned. 'Then back to the office. I dread to think what's been going on while we've been away.'

Laughing, they finished their drinks. Blake's desk was piled high with paperwork and he looked anxiously at Emma as they entered.

'Hello, Blake,' Emma spoke gently. 'It's good to be back.'

She gave him an encouraging smile and went to her desk. Time to let the past go, she thought. No joy would come from recriminations; and by the look on Blake's face, he felt enough guilt for his crimes.

*　*　*

The next few weeks passed in a haze of happiness. Although Alex was still inclined to be moody, he hadn't retracted his declaration of love, and

183

they worked side by side, Emma with joy in her heart and Alex warmly attentive most of the time. Tony, much to Emma's delight, had decided to invest in Leigh Manor, and his frequent visits livened the dinner table.

Today, Tony and Celia were coming, once again, for the weekend. As she worked, Emma had one eye on the open window, waiting for the sound of their car on the gravel. It was towards evening when she finally heard them arrive and she ran into the hall.

'Celia.' She clasped her friend in her arms. 'How lovely to see you.' She grabbed her case as Alex greeted Tony. 'Come on up and let's catch up on the gossip.'

The evening passed pleasantly, and the next morning saw Tony and Alex disappearing into Alex's study. 'We've business to discuss,' Alex said abruptly in answer to Emma's query, and she was perturbed to notice a frown on his brow.

'Serious?' she asked lightly.

He stared at her for a moment, his dark eyes brooding, and then smiled slightly. 'Never you mind; nothing to worry about.'

Emma was irritated by the frivolous comment; but as she and Celia set off for a walk in the warm sunshine, she forgot her annoyance.

'So tell me,' Emma said as she slid her arm through Celia's, 'how are things between you and Tony?'

Celia looked thoughtful for a moment as she gazed at the hazy hills in the distance. 'I think they might be serious,' she said at last.

'Oh?'

'I haven't felt this way about a man before,' Celia conceded. 'We really get on wonderfully well, and we have so many interests in common. And,' she added, grinning mischievously, 'he's tremendously attractive!'

'Oh Celia, I'm so glad for you.' Emma gave her friend's arm a squeeze.

'And you and Alex?' Celia neatly turned the conversation.

Emma sighed happily. 'I'm so happy, Celia. Like you, I really think I've found the right man at last.'

'Nothing more from Frank?'

Emma shook her head. 'Nothing from Diane either, thank goodness. I gather from Janet that Diane is spending quite a lot of time in London, with Frank. Can you imagine?'

Celia shuddered. 'What a pair!'

They walked in companionable silence for a while.

'Let's go and have lunch in Kestleigh,' Emma suggested.

'That's a lovely idea,' Celia agreed.

By contrast, dinner that evening was a sombre affair. Both Tony and Alex were quiet and seemed deep in thought. The women chattered away, but Emma looked at Alex anxiously. There was something wrong, she just knew it.

11

The next day Tony and Celia departed early, and Alex shut himself in the study, not emerging until evening. 'I'm going to London tomorrow,' he said abruptly as Janet served dinner.

'By yourself?' Emma was startled.

Alex nodded, but his dark eyes were brooding as he stared over her shoulder through the window. 'I've some business to sort out.'

'What is it, Alex?' Emma asked gently. 'What's wrong?'

'Nothing's wrong.' He sounded irritated. 'I don't have to tell you everything, Emma.'

His words stung, and they finished their meal in silence. She rose and turned to go. 'What time are you leaving?' she asked, her voice coolly polite.

He came round the table and pulled her stiff body into his arms. 'I'm sorry,

Emma,' he said huskily against her hair. 'I didn't mean to upset you, but there's something I've got to sort out for myself. I promise I'll tell you all about it when I get back.'

'How long will you be away?'

'A few days.'

Her heart sank. 'Well, I'll try and be patient.' She pulled away and managed a small smile. 'Just remember I love you, Alex.'

She left the room before he could see her tears, and dawn was breaking when she heard his car pull away down the lane.

* * *

The days were difficult. Emma tried not to worry, and immersed herself in work. Thankfully, Leigh Leisure was sailing along.

She spent some time rekindling her easy working relationship with Blake. Now that he had recovered from his self-recriminatory period, he proved to be the good manager Alex had always maintained he was, and he had sought help for his addiction. Ever cheerful, he was now out to prove he could be trusted again.

★　★　★

At last the message came from Alex that he was on his way home. Waking early that morning to the birds singing in the sparkling sunshine, Emma washed quickly, and throwing a cardigan over her shoulders, set off down the lane. The hedgerows glittered with dew, and wild vetches bobbed in the grasses. She took a deep breath of the scented air and leaned over the gate, smiling as she saw Jumbo in the distance.

The bull ambled across the field, stopping now and then to twist his tongue around a bunch of grass. Eventually he stood in front of her, staring at her. He blew through his nose and butted the gate.

'Alex is coming home,' she informed

him, her heart beating rapidly.

At that moment she heard the sound of a car. Her heart leapt as she turned and the BMW rounded the corner. Pulling to a halt, a grinning Alex emerged.

'Don't tell me I've got to rescue you again,' he teased.

Emma laughed and ran into his arms. 'Yes, please,' she begged.

He kissed her soundly and she felt the familiar curling in her stomach.

'Oh Alex, it's good to see you back,' she said at last. 'I didn't expect you yet.'

He leaned on the gate and stared at his bull. 'I couldn't sleep,' he said quietly. 'I suddenly thought, 'This is ridiculous, I may as well drive home.' So here I am.'

'Business successful?' Emma asked casually.

She heard Alex take a deep breath. 'I saw my mother,' he said abruptly.

'Oh!' was all Emma could manage. 'And?' she added, as Alex remained silent.

'It was painful.'

'Yes.'

'Tony traced her for me. He was determined.'

'That's Tony. Very determined.' Emma smiled.

'We had a long talk. She was as shocked as I was by the meeting.'

Emma waited as Jumbo stood silently, staring at them as if he too were aware of the tension.

Alex ran his fingers absently along Jumbo's nose. 'Apparently Tony was right — my mother found my father too difficult to live with. She had a breakdown. When she recovered, my father had made all the arrangements for her to live away, with an allowance, as long as she didn't contact me again. He persuaded her that I needed the security and stability that only he could give.'

'Your father thought he was doing what was best for you?'

Alex shrugged. 'I expect so.' He gave a wry smile. 'Anyway, we've made our peace. She has a fashion shop that she's built into a thriving business, and she seems to have been reasonably happy.'

'A fashion shop?' Emma's eyes lit up.

'In Woking. She's doing very well.'

'I'm glad to hear it.'

'I'll take you to see her one day.'

'I'd like that,' Emma said quietly.

They stood in silence for a moment.

'Alex . . . ' Emma hesitated. 'Do you think, now, maybe you'll learn to trust women?'

'It'll take some practice,' he teased. 'But, yes.' His expression sobered. 'I feel as if a great weight's been lifted off me. I seemed to be carrying a great lump of anger around in my heart, and that stopped any loving emotion penetrating my defences.'

'So you'll be more tolerant and easygoing?' Emma was laughing. 'That'll be something to experience!'

He grabbed her arm and pulled her towards him. 'More loving, certainly.' He placed a kiss on her quivering lips. 'But easy-going?' He smiled. 'That'd be too much to expect. Especially in the office. We have a huge profit to make, and don't you forget it.'

'As if I could.' Emma sighed and nestled up against him. 'But oh, Alex, it's so lovely to see you laughing and happy.'

He looked down at her in silence, his black eyes deep with longing. 'Yes, Emma,' he said softly. 'I'm happy; happier than I ever dreamed possible. With you by my side, we'll conquer the world. Well, some of it anyway.'

'We'll conquer our own little world, Alex. I promise.'

'I do love you, you know.' His serious eyes probed hers for a long moment.

'I love you too, Alex.' She reached towards him as he bent his lips to hers.

They stood, locked in a cocoon of emotion, until the sound of the gate rattling made Alex pull away, laughing. 'Let's get back to Leigh Manor,' he said gruffly. 'I missed my breakfast and I'm starving!'

Jumbo pawed the gate and Emma chuckled. 'See you later, Jumbo,' she called as she slipped into the car. As they sped away, Jumbo snorted happily and foraged in the grass.

* * *

'I thought we'd take Tony and Celia out to dinner,' Alex said later that week. 'To say thank you. They've proved to be wonderful friends.'

'That's a lovely idea,' Emma said. 'Are they coming down this weekend?'

Alex nodded. 'Tony wants to see how Dan's progressing, and I've suggested they stay the night.'

'Great.'

* * *

Saturday dawned bright and sunny, and Emma and Celia roamed in the gardens and caught up on news as Tony and Alex discussed business. It was a happy foursome that sat down to dinner that night. They had booked the best table in The Jolly Duck, and Alex had ordered champagne.

Then, suddenly, Emma let out a gasp as the door of the restaurant opened behind them. As the others followed her stare, they saw Frank and Diane enter. 'Oh, damn,' Tony muttered.

The pair started to weave through the tables, and then Diane spotted them. Turning to Frank, she whispered in his ear. Frank glared angrily in their direction and took a step towards them. He tried to brush off Diane's restraining hand, and then she swung him round and there was a heated exchange of words. For a moment Frank seemed undecided; and then, without further ado and with their noses in the air, the pair stormed out.

Alex let out a sigh of relief. 'I must admit Frank looked rather annoyed,' he said drily. 'I had a feeling we were in for a confrontation.'

'Oh, didn't I tell you?' Emma said, an innocent expression on her face. 'After the rumpus over the cheque, I popped it in my bag while I considered the situation. I banked it the other day.'

Alex looked at Emma incredulously. 'You did?'

She smiled. 'He did try to con us

after all, and what's sauce for the goose . . . '

A cheer echoed around the table. The shadows of the past had left with Frank and Diane, and the future beckoned invitingly.

'To Leigh Manor and all who prosper with her.' Alex raised his glass, and the bubbles sparkled in the gentle light.

'To Leigh Manor,' Emma repeated.

Tony proposed another toast.

'To Alex and Emma,' he said quietly.

We do hope that you have enjoyed reading this large print book.

Did you know that all of our titles are available for purchase?

We publish a wide range of high quality large print books including:
Romances, Mysteries, Classics
General Fiction
Non Fiction and Westerns

Special interest titles available in large print are:
The Little Oxford Dictionary
Music Book, Song Book
Hymn Book, Service Book

Also available from us courtesy of Oxford University Press:
Young Readers' Dictionary
(large print edition)
Young Readers' Thesaurus
(large print edition)

For further information or a free brochure, please contact us at:
Ulverscroft Large Print Books Ltd.,
The Green, Bradgate Road, Anstey,
Leicester, LE7 7FU, England.
Tel: (00 44) 0116 236 4325
Fax: (00 44) 0116 234 0205

FALLING FOR DR. RIGHT

Jo Bartlett

In the wake of her mother's death and a broken engagement, Dr. Evie Daniels decides to travel the world, doing everything her mum never had the chance to. Leaving her London job, she accepts a temporary locum position in the remote Scottish town of Balloch Pass, where she finds herself enjoying the work and community — and her handsome colleague Dr. Alasdair James. The feeling is mutual — but Alasdair is bound to Balloch Pass, whilst Evie is committed to spreading her wings . . .

THE ART OF LOVE

Anne Holman

Hazel Crick is furious when her entry for the Town Art Show is rejected. Convinced her colleague Jon Hunter is responsible, she accuses him of vetoing her painting out of spite. Later that day, she waits beside Jon's car to apologise. But this puts her in the wrong place at the wrong time: she is grabbed, bound, gagged, and bundled into Jon's car — unbeknownst to him. The two are about to be flung together in a hair-raising European adventure . . .

A GERMAN SUMMER

Carol MacLean

When her younger sister Stella disappears, it's up to Jo to find her and bring her home. It soon becomes clear that Stella has gone to Germany to stay with Jo's childhood penpal Max, with whom she has secretly been corresponding. As the sisters enjoy Max's hospitality in his splendid castle, Jo discovers that the grown-up man is very different to the boy she once knew — and very attractive, too. But staying in Germany is not an option, especially when her ill mother needs her back home . . .

LOVE'S LANGUAGE

Sarah Purdue

Sophie Carson has always dreamed of being a teacher, and now finally she has the chance. Due to start her training in Wales, there is only one problem: she must be able to read and write in Welsh. While studying, she works at the caravan site in Anglesey previously owned by her grandparents — and meets David, the heartbroken son of the new owners. Can Sophie convince him to help her with her studies, as she tries to help him mend his broken heart?